The History of King Leir: A Retelling

David Bruce

Published by David Bruce, 2022.

THE HISTORY OF KING LEIR: A RETELLING

First edition. July 11, 2022.

Copyright © 2022 David Bruce.

ISBN: 979-8201051334

Written by David Bruce.

Dedication

Dedicated to Carl Eugene Bruce and Josephine Saturday Bruce

My father, Carl Eugene Bruce, died on 24 October 2013. He used to work for Ohio Power, and at one time, his job was to shut off the electricity of people who had not paid their bills. He sometimes would find a home with an impoverished mother and some children. Instead of shutting off their electricity, he would tell the mother that she needed to pay her bill or soon her electricity would be shut off. He would write on a form that no one was home when he stopped by because if no one was home he did not have to shut off their electricity.

The best good deed that anyone ever did for my father occurred after a storm that knocked down many power lines. He and other linemen worked long hours and got wet and cold. Their feet were freezing because water got into their boots and soaked their socks. Fortunately, a kind woman gave my father and the other linemen dry socks to wear.

My mother, Josephine Saturday Bruce, died on 14 June 2003. She used to work at a store that sold clothing. One day, an impoverished mother with a baby clothed in rags walked into the store and started shoplifting in an interesting way: The mother took the rags off her baby and dressed the infant in new clothing. My mother knew that this mother could not afford to buy the clothing, but she helped the mother dress her baby and then she watched as the mother walked out of the store without paying.

***

The doing of good deeds is important. As a free person, you can choose to live your life as a good person or as a bad person. To be a good person, do good deeds. To be a bad person, do bad deeds. If you do good deeds, you will become good. If you do bad deeds, you will become bad. To become the person you want to be, act as if you already are that kind of person. Each of us chooses what kind of person we will become. To become a good person, do the things a good person does. To become a bad person, do the things a bad person does. The opportunity to take action to become the kind of person you want to be is yours.

Human beings have free will. According to the Babylonian Niddah 16b, whenever a baby is to be conceived, the Lailah (angel in charge of contraception) takes the drop of semen that will result in the conception and asks God, "Sovereign of the Universe, what is going to be the fate of this drop? Will it develop into a robust or into a weak person? An intelligent or a stupid person? A wealthy or a poor person?" The Lailah asks all these questions, but it does not ask, "Will it develop into a righteous or a wicked person?" The answer to that question lies in the decisions to be freely made by the human being that is the result of the conception.

A Buddhist monk visiting a class wrote this on the chalkboard: "EVERYONE WANTS TO SAVE THE WORLD, BUT NO ONE WANTS TO HELP MOM DO THE DISHES." The students laughed, but the monk then said, "Statistically, it's highly unlikely that any of you will ever have the opportunity to run into a burning orphanage and rescue an infant. But, in the smallest gesture of kindness — a warm smile, holding the door for the person behind you, shoveling the driveway of the elderly person next door — you have committed an act of immeasurable profundity, because to each of us, our life is our universe."

In her book titled *I Have Chosen to Stay and Fight*, comedian Margaret Cho writes, "I believe that we get complimentary snack-size portions of the afterlife, and we all receive them in a different way." For Ms. Cho, many of her snack-size portions of the afterlife come in hip hop music. Other people get different snack-size portions of the afterlife, and we all must be on the lookout for them when they come our way. And perhaps doing good deeds and experiencing good deeds are snack-size portions of the afterlife.

COVER PHOTO for *The History of King Leir*: A Retelling: https://pixabay.com/en/old-man-male-face-beard-portrait-3102577/

Educate yourself.
Read like a wolf eats.
Books then, books now, books forever
Be excellent to each other.

In this retelling, as in all my retellings, I have tried to make the work of literature accessible to modern readers who may lack some of the knowledge about mythology, religion, and history that the literary work's contemporary audience had.

Do you know a language other than English? If you do, I give you permission to translate this book, copyright your translation, publish or self-publish it, and keep all the royalties for yourself. (Do give me credit, of course, for the original retelling.)

I would like to see my retellings of classic literature used in schools, so I give permission to the country of Finland (and all other countries) to give copies of this book to all students forever. I also give permission to the state of Texas (and all other states) to give copies of this book to all students forever. I also give permission to all teachers to give copies of this book to all students forever.

Teachers need not actually teach my retellings. Teachers are welcome to give students copies of my eBooks as background material. For example, if they are teaching Homer's *Iliad* and *Odyssey*, teachers are welcome to give students copies of my *Virgil's* Aeneid: *A Retelling in Prose* and tell students, "Here's another ancient epic you may want to read in your spare time."

CAST OF CHARACTERS

(In order of appearance)

Leir, King of Britain. Parts of Britain had other kings; Leir was king of the area around Troynovant, an early name for London.

Skalliger, a nobleman in King Leir's court.

A Nobleman.

Perillus, a nobleman, follower of King Leir. Like Leir, he is an old man.

Gonorill, daughter of King Leir, later wife of the King of Cornwall. Gonorill is Leir's oldest daughter.

Ragan, daughter of King Leir, later wife of the King of Cambria. Ragan is Leir's middle daughter.

Cordella, daughter of King Leir, later wife of the King of Gallia. Cordella is Leir's youngest daughter.

King of Gallia.

Mumford, follower of the King of Gallia.

Noblemen.

King of Cornwall.

King of Cornwall's Servant.

King of Cambria. His name is Morgan.

King of Cambria's Servant.

Messenger. Potential murderer.

Ambassador, from Gaul.

First Mariner.

Second Mariner.

First Captain.

First Watchman.

Second Watchman.

Second Captain.

ALTERNATE CAST OF CHARACTERS

FEMALE CHARACTERS

Gonorill, daughter of King Leir, later wife of the King of Cornwall.

Ragan, daughter of King Leir, later wife of the King of Cambria.

Cordella, daughter of King Leir, later wife of the King of Gallia.

MALE CHARACTERS

Leir, King of Britain.

King of Cornwall.

King of Cambria.

Skalliger, a nobleman in King Leir's court.

Perillus, a nobleman, follower of King Leir.

King of Gaul.

Mumford, follower of the King of Gallia.

Ambassador, from Gaul.

Servant, of the King of Cornwall.

Servant, of the King of Cambria.

Messenger (Potential Murderer).

Two Mariners.

Captain of the Watch.

Two Watchmen.

Two Captains.

MINOR CHARACTERS

Noblemen, Messengers, Citizens.

CHAPTER 1

— 1.1 —

— Scene 1 —

King Leir, Skalliger, Perillus, and another nobleman were talking together in King Leir's presence-chamber. Skalliger and Perillus were two noblemen who were advisers to the king.

Using the royal plural, King Leir said, "As befits our grief, the funeral rites have been performed of our too recently deceased and dearest queen, whose soul, I hope, possessed of Heavenly joys, rides in triumph among the cherubim.

"Let us request your grave advice, my lords, about finding husbands for our princely daughters, for whom our care is specially employed, in accordance with natural law, to advance their states in marriage with some royal mates. As their father, I naturally want to find good husbands for them.

"Now they are lacking their mother's good advice, under whose government they have received a perfect pattern and role model of a virtuous life — my daughters are left, as it were, like a ship without a stern, or like helpless sheep without a pastor's care."

Still using the royal plural, he said, "Although we ourselves do dearly cherish them, yet we are ignorant of their affairs, for fathers best know how to govern sons, but the mother's counsel turns daughters' steps. Fathers guide sons, while mothers guide daughters.

"We lack a son to inherit our crown, and the course of time has cancelled the chance of further issue from our withered loins. I am too old to have any more children. One foot of mine already hangs in the grave, and age has made deep furrows in my face.

"The world is weary of me, and I am weary of the world. I would gladly relinquish these earthly cares and think upon the welfare of my soul, which by no better means may be effected than by relinquishing the crown from me in equal dowry to my three daughters."

3

Skalliger said, "This is a worthy concern, my liege, which well declares the ardent love you bore to our former queen. And since your grace has given me permission to speak, I say that this is what I think: Your majesty, knowing well what various suitors your princely daughters have, should give them each a dowry — more or less, as is their worth — to them who profess to love you."

King Leir said, "No more nor less, but even all alike. My love for my daughters is fixed. It is all fashioned in one mold, and therefore my judgment shall be impartial. Both old and young shall have an equal dowry from me."

"My gracious lord," a nobleman said, "I heartily wish that God had lent you a male heir whose heritage is undoubted, who might have sat upon your royal throne when Fates should loose the prison of your life and let you die. With the succession of an undoubted heir, all this doubt might cease and, as by you, by him we might have peace.

"But after-wishes always come too late and nothing can revoke the course of fate. Therefore, my liege, my opinion deems it best to match in marriage your daughters with some of your neighboring kings whose kingdoms border our kingdom within the bounds of Albion: the island of Britain. By means of the united friendship of these neighboring kings, our state may be protected against all foreign hate."

King Leir said, "Herein, my lords, your wishes agree with mine, and mine, I hope, do agree with Heavenly powers, for at this instant two near-neighboring kings — the King of Cornwall and the King of Cambria — propose love and marriage to two of my daughters: Gonorill and Ragan.

"My youngest daughter, fair Cordella, vows not to like a monarch unless love allows it. Several peers have solicited her for marriage, but her discriminating desire hears none of them. She will not marry someone whom she does not love.

"Yet, if my cunning policy may beguile her, I'll match her in marriage to some king within this isle and so establish such a perfect peace as Fortune's force shall never be strong enough to make it cease."

Perillus said, "Of us and ours, your gracious care, my lord, deserves an everlasting memory to be enrolled in historical chronicles of fame by never-dying perpetuity. Yet, to become so provident a prince, do not lose the title of a loving father. Do not force love where fancy cannot dwell, lest streams, being dammed up, above the banks do swell."

King Leir said, "I am resolved and have made up my mind, and even now my mind meditates on a sudden, previously unthought-of stratagem to test which of my daughters loves me best, which, until I know, I cannot be in rest.

"This granted, when they jointly shall contend, each to exceed the other in their love, then at the right moment I will take Cordella, even as she protests that she loves me best.

"I'll say, 'Then, daughter, grant me one request: To show you love me as your sisters do, accept a husband whom I myself will persuade to marry you.'

"Once I say this, she cannot well deny my suit, although, poor soul, her senses will be mute. Then I will triumph in my cunning strategy, and match her in marriage with a king of another part of Britain."

Skalliger thought, *I'll go to your two oldest daughters ahead of time and betray your secret plot.*

Perillus thought, *Thus, fathers think to beguile their children, and they themselves often first repent when Heavenly powers frustrate their intent.*

— 1.2 —

— Scene 2 —

Gonorill and Ragan talked together in a room of King Leir's palace.

Gonorill said, "I marvel, Ragan, how you can endure to see that proud pert peat — spoiled brat — our youngest sister, Cordella, value so slightly us, her elders, as if we were no better than herself!

"We cannot have a quaint device — a fashionable trinket — or a new-made fashion of our own sophisticated devising, but if she likes it, she will quickly have the same, or work to acquire something newer that will exceed us both.

"Besides, she is so nice and refined and so demure, so sober, courteous, modest, and precise, that all the court has work enough to do to talk about how she exceeds both me and you."

Some of these words had both a positive and a negative meaning. Of course, "nice" has a positive meaning, but it can also mean "extravagant." The word "precise" means "fastidious," but it was also used to refer to Puritans' overly fastidious piety.

Ragan said, "What should I do? I wish it were in my power to find a cure for this contagious ill. Some desperate medicine — an extreme remedy — must be soon applied to dim the glory of her mounting fame, or else, before much longer, she'll have both prick and praise, and we must be set by for working days. We will be treated as if we are ordinary laborers."

The "prick" is the highest point; in this context, it means status and prestige above that of Cordella's older sisters: Gonorill and Ragan. "Prick" also means "bull's-eye," and "prick and praise" means "goal."

Ragan continued, "Do you not see how great a choice of suitors she daily has, and of the best degree and highest rank? Say, among all of her suitors, she happens to fancy one and have a husband when we have none. Why, then, by right, to her we must give place, although it would be ever so much to our disgrace."

If Cordella were to marry first, before Gonorill and Ragan, she would have a higher social standing than they, although they are older than she is.

Gonorill said, "By my virginity, rather than she shall have a husband before me, I'll marry one or other man in his shirt."

To marry someone in his shirt means to marry very quickly, when the groom is figuratively only partially dressed.

She added, "And yet I have made half a grant already of my good will to the King of Cornwall. I have half agreed to marry him."

For Gonorill to marry the King of Cornwall, she would need her father's consent. She had already indicated her interest in marrying the King of Cornwall, but the negotiations for marriage were not fully completed.

Skalliger walked quickly toward them.

Ragan said, "Swear not so deeply, sister. Here comes my Lord Skalliger. His haste in coming to us implies that he has something important to tell us."

Skalliger said, "Sweet princesses, I am glad I met you here so luckily. I have good news that concerns you both and needs speedy action."

Ragan said, "For God's sake, tell us what it is, my lord! I am with child until you utter it."

Ragan was not literally pregnant. She was speaking metaphorically. A pregnant woman often has cravings, and Ragan craved to quickly hear the news.

Ragan's "I am with child" meant "I am filled with longing."

Skalliger said to Ragan, "Madam, to satisfy your longing, this is the news: Your father, in great secrecy, today told me he means to marry you immediately to the noble Prince of Cambria."

He said to Gonorill, "You, madam, he means to marry to the King of Cornwall."

He then said to both sisters, "He would happily marry your younger sister to the rich King of Hibernia."

Hibernia is the name of Ireland in classical Latin.

Skalliger added, "But he fears she will hardly consent, for hitherto she never could fancy him. If she does yield and marry him, why then, he will divide his kingdom among you three for your dowries. But yet there is a further mystery that, as long as you will keep it a secret, I will disclose."

Gonorill said, "Whatever you speak to us, kind Skalliger, think that you are speaking it only to yourself."

Skalliger said, "He earnestly wants to know which of you three bear him the most love, and he so extremely dotes on and unreasonably esteems your loves as never any person did, I think, before.

"He immediately intends to send for you to be resolved of this tormenting doubt, and whatever persons' answer pleases him the best, they shall have the most dowry for their marriages."

Ragan said, "Oh, I wish that I had some pleasing mermaid's voice that I could use to enchant his senseless senses!"

She was thinking of the classical sweet-singing Sirens that lured sailors to their death.

Skalliger said, "Because he supposes that Cordella, striving to go beyond you in her love, will promise to do whatever he desires, he plans to then immediately bind her with an oath, for his sake, to take the Hibernian king in marriage.

"This is the sum of all I have to say, which, now that I am done, I humbly take my leave, not doubting that your wisdoms will foresee which course will lead to the best results for you."

"Thanks, gentle Skalliger," Gonorill said. "Your kindness, which we don't deserve, shall not be unrequited, if we live."

Skalliger exited.

"Now we have a suitable occasion offered to us to be revenged — unperceived — upon Cordella," Ragan said.

"Indeed, the revenge we will inflict on her shall be thought of as piety in us," Gonorill said.

If all worked out well for Gonorill and Ragan, they would be thought to be devoted daughters as they criticized their younger sister, Cordella.

Gonorill continued, "I will so flatter my doting father as he was never so flattered in his life. Indeed, I will say that if it is his pleasure to marry me to a beggar, I will yield and marry the beggar — because I know, whatever I say to him, that he intends to marry me to the King of Cornwall."

"I'll say the same," Ragan said, "for I am well assured, whatever I say to please the mind of the old man, who dotes as if he were a child again, I shall enjoy the noble Cambrian prince.

"Just to feed his humor, it will suffice to say that I am happy with anyone to whom he'll marry me. This will please him more than Apollo's music ever pleased Jove."

Apollo is the god of music and master of the lyre; Jove is Jupiter, king of the gods.

Gonorill said, "I smile to think in what a woeful plight Cordella will be when we answer thus, for she will rather die than give her consent to join in marriage with the Irish king. So our father will think she does not love him because she will not grant his desire.

"This argument we will aggravate in such bitter terms that he will soon convert his love for her to hatred for her, for he, you know, is always in extremes."

Ragan said, "No one in all the world could lay a better plot; I can't wait until it is put in practice."

— 1.3 —
— Scene 3 —

In the king's presence-chamber, King Leir and Perillus talked together.

King Leir ordered, "Perillus, go and seek my daughters. Command them to immediately come and speak with me."

"I will, my gracious lord," Perillus replied and exited.

King Leir said to himself, "Oh, what a combat feels my panting heart between children's love and care of the public good. How dear my daughters are to my soul none knows but He Who knows my thoughts and secret deeds.

"Ah, little do they know the dear regard and great importance wherein I hold their future state to come. When they securely sleep

9

on beds of down, these aged eyes of mine stay awake and watch out for their good. While they, like difficult-to-manage children, engage in youthful amusements, this throbbing heart is pierced with dire annoyances.

"Just as the sun exceeds the smallest star, by so much the father's love exceeds the child's. Yet my complaints are causeless, for the world does not yield children more compliant than mine are, and yet I think my mind still foretells I know not what, and I fear some ill."

Perillus returned, leading King Leir's three daughters: Gonorill, Ragan, and Cordella.

King Leir said, "Well, here my daughters come. I have found out an immediate means to rid me of this fear I am feeling."

Gonorill said, "Our royal lord and father, in all duty we come to know the nature of your will and why you so hastily have sent for us."

King Leir replied, "Dear Gonorill, kind Ragan, sweet Cordella, you flourishing branches of a kingly stock, sprung from a tree that once did flourish green, but whose blossoms now are nipped with winter's frost, with pale, grim Death waiting upon my steps and summoning me to his next court day — my day of judgment.

"Therefore, dear daughters, as you value the safety of him who was the cause of your first being, resolve a doubt that much molests my mind: Which of you three to me would prove to be kindest, which loves me most, and which, at my request, will soonest yield to their father's command?"

Gonorill said, "I hope my gracious father has no doubt of any of his daughters' love to him, yet, for my part, to show my zeal to you, which cannot be in windy words and fatuous language recited, I prize my love to you at such a rate that I think my life inferior to my love. If you were to tell me to tie a millstone about my neck and leap into the sea, at your command I willingly would do it."

Matthew 18:6 states, "*But whosoever shall offend one of these little ones which believe in me, it were better for him, that a millstone were hanged about his neck, and that he were drowned in the depth of the sea"* (1599 Geneva Bible).

Cordella, the youngest daughter, sincerely believed in God.

Gonorill continued, "Indeed, in order to do you good, I would climb the highest turret in all Britain, and from the top I would leap headfirst to the ground.

Luke 4:9-12 (1599 Geneva Bible) states this:

9 Then he [the devil] brought him [Jesus] to Jerusalem, and set him on a pinnacle of the Temple, and said unto him, If thou be the Son of God, cast thyself down from hence,

10 For it is written, That he will give his Angels charge over thee to keep thee:

11 And with their hands they shall lift thee up, lest at anytime thou shouldest dash thy foot against a stone.

12 And Jesus answered, and said unto him, It is said, Thou shalt not tempt the Lord thy God.

Gonorill continued, "Indeed, more, should you engage me to marry the lowest and basest person in all the spacious world, without reply I would do it.

"In brief, command whatever you desire, and if I fail to obey you, I require no favor."

King Leir replied, "Oh, how your words revive my dying soul!"

Cordella thought, *Oh, how I hate this flattery!*

King Leir said, "But what does Ragan say in answer to her father's question?"

Ragan replied, "Oh, I wish that my simple utterance could suffice to tell you the true intention of my heart, which burns in zeal of duty to your grace and can never be quenched except by my desire to show the same in outward zealousness.

"Oh, I wish that there were some other maiden who dared to make a challenge of her love with me. I'd make her soon confess that she never loved her father half as well as I do you.

"Yes, then my deeds should prove more straightforwardly how much my zeal abounds to your grace. But, for them all, let this one example suffice to ratify my love before your eyes: I have very noble suitors to my love, no worse than kings, and happily I love one, yet if you wanted me to make my choice anew, I'd bridle my own desire, and I would be ruled by you. I would marry the man you wanted me to marry."

King Leir asked rhetorically about Ragan's words, "Did Philomela ever sing so sweet a note?"

Philomela was a mortal woman who was turned into a sweet-singing nightingale. Her sister's husband, Tereus, raped her and cut out her tongue so that she could not tell anyone that he had raped her. Philomela wove a tapestry, however, that revealed the rape and rapist. She gave the tapestry to her sister, Procne, who killed her son by Tereus, cooked him, and fed him to Tereus. When Tereus learned that he had eaten the flesh of his son, he pursued Procne and Philomela, intending to kill them. They prayed to the gods to change them into birds, and the gods answered the prayer, transforming Procne into a swallow and Philomela into a nightingale.

Cordella thought about Ragan's words, *Did any flatterer ever tell so false a tale?*

King Leir said, "Speak now, Cordella, make my joys at their fullest, and drop down nectar from your honey lips."

Cordella replied, "I cannot paint my duty forth in words; I hope my deeds shall make report for me. But look what love the child owes the father: The same love to you I bear, my gracious lord."

Gonorill said to Cordella, "Here is an answer answerless indeed! If you were my daughter, I would scarcely tolerate it."

Ragan said to Cordella, "Don't you blush, proud peacock as you are, to make our father such a slight, flimsy, weak reply?"

King Leir said to Cordella, "Why, how now, 'minion,' are you grown so proud?"

A minion is a darling, a favorite; unfortunately, King Leir was using the word sarcastically.

He continued, "Does our dear love make you thus imperious? Has your love become so small toward us that you scorn to tell us what it is? Do you love us as every child loves his or her father? True, indeed — you love us as some who by disobedience shorten their fathers' days, and so would you; some are so father-sick that they make means to rid their fathers from the world, and so would you; some are indifferent whether their aged parents live or die, and so are you.

"But if you knew, proud girl, what care and concern I had to foster you to this point in your life, ah, then you would say as your sisters do: 'Our life is less valuable than the love we owe to you.'"

Cordella said, "Dear father, do not so mistake my words, nor let my plain meaning be misconstrued. My tongue was never used in flattery."

Gonorill said, "You had best not say I flatter. If you do, my deeds shall show I don't flatter with you. I love my father better than you can."

Cordella said, "That praise of yourself would be great, if it were spoken from another's mouth and not by you, but it seems your neighbors dwell far off since it is you and not they who speak your praise."

Ragan said, "Here is one who will confirm as much as she has said, both for myself and her. I say that you do not wish my father's good."

Cordella began, "Dear father —"

Her father, King Leir, interrupted, "Silence, bastard imp — you are no child of King Leir! I will not hear you speak one tiny tittle more. Don't call me 'father' if you love your life, nor even once presume to call Gonorill and Ragan your sisters.

"Look for no help henceforth from me or mine. Shift for yourself as you will, and trust to yourself. Manage your life without my help.

"I will equally divide my kingdom between your two sisters to be their royal dowry, and I will bestow these halves of my kingdom as your sisters' worthy deserts.

"Once this is done, so that you shall not have the hope to have a child's part of my possessions and power in the time to come, I immediately will dispossess myself of my possessions and power and set your sisters upon my princely throne."

"I always thought that pride would have a fall," Gonorill said.

"Plain-dealing and plain-speaking sister," Ragan said sarcastically, "your beauty is so resplendent that you need no dowry to make you a queen."

King Leir, Gonorill, and Ragan exited.

Cordella said, "Now whither — poor, forsaken — shall I go, when my own sisters triumph in my woe, but to Him Who protects the just? In Him will poor Cordella put her trust. These hands shall labor in order to get money for my spending, and so I'll live until my days have ending."

She exited.

Perillus said to himself, "Oh, how I grieve to see my lord so foolish as to dote so much upon vain flattering words. Ah, if he had only with good advice weighed the hidden content of her humble speech, reason would not have given place to rage, nor would poor Cordella have suffered such disgrace."

CHAPTER 2

— 2.1 —

— Scene 4 —

The King of Gallia spoke with Mumford and three other of his nobles.

The King of Gallia said, "Attempt no longer to dissuade me, my lords, I am resolved with the next fair wind to sail for Britain in some disguise in order to see whether swift-spreading rumor is too extravagant in the wondrous praise of these three nymphs: the daughters of King Leir.

"If my then-present view matches the absent praise, and my eyes allow that what our ears have heard is true, and Venus, goddess of love, stands auspicious to my vows and wishes me well and if Fortune favors what I take in hand, I will return in possession of as rich a prize as Jason when he with the help of his Argonauts won the Golden Fleece."

Mumford said, "May the Heavens grant you may. The match would be full of honor and well befitting the young Gallian king.

"I wish that your grace would favor me so much as to make me partner of your pilgrimage. I long to see the attractive British dames and feed my eyes upon their rare perfections, for until I know the contrary, I'll say that our dames in France are more beautiful than the British women are."

"Lord Mumford," the King of Gallia said, "you have saved me a labor in offering that which I did mean to ask you, and I most willingly accept your company. Yet, first I will command you to observe some few conditions that I shall propose."

Mumford replied, "As long as you do not keep my eyes from looking after the amorous glances of fair dames, and as long as you do not keep my tongue from speaking, my lips from kissing when occasion serves, my hands from making French salutations, and my knees from bowing to gallant girls — obeying such commands would be a task harder than flesh and blood is able to endure — command what else you please, and I will rest content."

The King of Gallia said, "To bind you from a thing you can not leave would be only a means to make you seek it more, and therefore speak, look, kiss, and salute for me; in doing these things I myself am likely to second you.

"Now hear your task: I charge you, from the time that first we set sail for the British shore, to use no words to me that would reveal that I am a king, but in the friendliest manner that you can, treat me as your companion, for we will go disguised in palmers' clothing so that no man shall suspect who we are."

Palmers were religious pilgrims who had visited the Holy Land. Often they carried a palm leaf from the Holy Land. Often the palm leaf was folded into a cross.

"If that is all, I'll fit your turn and meet your requirements, I warrant you," Mumford said. "I am some kin to the Blunt family, and I think I am the bluntest of all my kindred; therefore, if I should be too blunt with you, thank yourself for asking me to be so."

"Your pleasant and humorous company will make the way seem short," the King of Gallia replied.

He then ordered the other nobles, "It remains that now in my absence from here I commit the government to you, my trusty lords and faithful councilors. Time cuts off the rest I have to say. The wind blows fair, and I must now go away."

The other noblemen said, "May the Heavens send your voyage to as good effect as we your land do purpose to protect. May your voyage have a good result."

— 2.2 —

— Scene 5 —

The King of Cornwall spoke with his manservant. He was wearing boots and spurs, and he carried in his hand a riding crop, aka whip, and

16

a letter. Apparently, he had received the letter and then immediately set out on a journey.

The King of Cornwall asked his manservant, "But how far distant are we from the court?"

"Some twenty miles, my lord, or thereabouts," his manservant replied.

"It seems to me twenty thousand miles," the King of Cornwall said, "yet I hope to be there within this hour."

The manservant thought, *Then you are likely to ride alone without me. I think my lord is weary of his life.*

A horse can travel twenty miles in two to four hours. If nothing else, the King of Cornwall seemed weary of his horse's life.

The King of Cornwall said, "Sweet Gonorill, I long to see your face, which has so kindly gratified and requited my love."

The King of Cambria arrived. Like the King of Cornwall, he was wearing boots and spurs, and he carried in his hand a riding crop, aka whip, and a letter. Like the King of Cornwall, he had apparently received the letter and then immediately set out on a journey. Like the King of Cornwall, he was accompanied by a manservant.

Looking at his letter, the King of Cambria said to his manservant, "Get a fresh horse, for by my soul I swear that I am past patience longer to do without the wished-for sight of my beloved mistress, dear Ragan, the stay and comfort of my life."

His manservant thought, *Now what in God's name does my lord intend to do? He thinks he never shall come at his journey's end. I wish that he had old Daedalus' waxen wings so that he might fly and therefore I might stay behind. For before we get to Troynovant, I see, he will quite tire himself, his horse, and me.*

Daedalus was a mythological figure who created wings made of feathers and wax so that he could fly away from the island of Crete, where he had been imprisoned. Daedalus' son, Icarus, was imprisoned with him and also flew away, but Icarus flew too high and got too close to the sun, which melted the wax of Icarus' wings, causing the feathers to fall off and Icarus to plunge into the sea, where he drowned.

Troynovant is New Troy, an old name for London. Some people believed that Brute, a descendant of the Trojan Aeneas, founded London.

The King of Cornwall and the King of Cambria looked at each other and were surprised to see each other.

The King of Cornwall said, "Brother of Cambria, we greet you well as one whom we little did expect to see here."

Male members of royalty often referred to each other as brothers.

The King of Cambria replied, "Brother of Cornwall, we have met each other at a fortuitous time. I thought as much to have met with the Sultan of Persia as to have met you in this place, my lord. No doubt it is about some great affairs that makes you come here so slenderly accompanied. You have only one manservant with you."

"To say the truth, my lord, it is no less," the King of Cornwall replied. "And, for your part, some hasty wind of chance has blown you hither thus upon the sudden."

"My lord, to break off further circumstances," the King of Cambria said, "for at this time I cannot endure delays, if you tell me your reason for being here, I will tell you mine."

"Indeed, I am happy to do so," the King of Cornwall replied, "and, therefore, to be brief, for I am sure my haste's as great as yours: I have been sent for to come to King Leir, who, by this letter, promises his eldest daughter, lovely Gonorill, to me in marriage and for immediate dowry the portion of half his territory and its associated rights. The lady's love I long ago possessed, but until now I never had the father's."

"You tell me wonders," the King of Cambria said, "yet I will relate strange news, and henceforth we must call each other brothers-in-law. Witness these lines in my letter."

He showed the letter to the King of Cornwall, and then continued, "Because of King Leir's honorable age and his being weary of the troubles of his crown, he will bestow on me in marriage his princely daughter Ragan, with half his territories and their associated revenues. I would have gladly married her with only one-third — not one-half — of his kingdom as dowry, such are her accomplishments."

The King of Cornwall said, "If I have one half and you have the other half, then between us we must necessarily have the whole."

"The hole!" the King of Cambria said. "What do you mean by that? By God's blood, I hope we shall have two holes between us."

He was referring to vaginas.

"Why, I mean the whole kingdom," the King of Cornwall replied.

"Yes, that's very true," the King of Cambria said.

"What then is left for his third daughter's dowry, lovely Cordella, whom the world admires?" the King of Cornwall asked.

"It is very strange," the King of Cambria said. "I don't know what to think, unless they intend to make a nun of her."

"It would be a pity for such rare beauty to be hidden within the compass of a cloister's wall," the King of Cornwall said, "but, howsoever, if King Leir's words prove to be true, it will be good, my lord, for me and you."

The King of Cambria replied, "Then let us hasten, all danger to prevent, for fear delays may alter his intent."

— 2.3 —

— Scene 6 —

Gonorill and Ragan talked together about Cordella.

Gonorill said, "Sister, when did you last see Cordella, that pretty piece who thinks no one is good enough to speak to her because sir-reverence, aka begging your pardon, she has a little extraordinary beauty?"

"Pretty piece" meaning "shrewd woman," but the phrase also has the connotation of "pretty piece of ass."

Ragan replied, "From the time my father ordered her to stay away from his presence, I have never seen her that I can remember. May God

19

give her joy of her surpassing beauty; I think her dowry will be small enough."

Gonorill said, "I have incensed my father so against her that he will never be reclaimed again. My father will not be able to reclaim the title of 'loving father' after the way he treated Cordella."

Both Ragan and Gonorill referred to King Leir as "my father" rather than "our father"; neither daughter was the sharing type.

"I was not much behind to do the like," Ragan said. "I helped."

Both Ragan and Gonorill believed and hoped that King Leir would never reverse his current bad opinion of Cordella.

"Indeed, sister, what moves you to bear her such 'good' will?" Gonorill asked.

"In truth, I think the same reason that moves you," Ragan said. "Because she surpasses us both in beauty."

"Beshrew your fingers, how right you can guess," Gonorill said. "I tell you truly, it cuts me to the heart."

Normally, the words "beshrew your fingers" mean "curse the actions of your fingers," but Gonorill had if anything been more eager to act evilly than Ragan. So, in this case, the phrase meant, "Damn you because you thought of the right reason — a reason that causes me pain."

Ragan said, "But we will keep her low enough, I warrant, and clip her wings for mounting up too high."

Clipping a bird's wings prevents it from flying.

Gonorill said sarcastically, "Whoever has her shall have a rich marriage of her."

"She would be a right fit to make a parson's wife," Ragan said, "for parsons, men say, do love fair women well, and many times do marry them with nothing."

"With no thing!" Gonorill said. "By the Virgin Mary, God forbid! Why, are there any such men?"

A "thing" is a penis. Gonorill had misunderstood — or pretended to misunderstand — Ragan.

"I mean, with no money," Ragan said.

"I beg your mercy, I much mistook you," Gonorill said. "And she is far too stately for the church: She'll lay her husband's benefice on her back even in one gown, if she may have her will."

Gonorill meant that Cordella would spend all of her parson husband's money on just one gown for her to wear.

"In faith, the poor soul, I pity her a little," Ragan said. "I wish that she were less beautiful or more fortunate. Well, I grow wearied until I see my Morgan, the gallant Prince of Cambria, arrive here."

"And so do I until the King of Cornwall presents himself to consummate my joys," Gonorill said. "Quiet, here comes my father."

"Consummate" meant "complete," but as used here also had a sense of sexual consummation.

King Leir, Perillus, and others entered the room.

Using the royal plural, King Leir said, "Cease, my good lords, and don't plead with me to reverse our censure that is now irrevocable. We have dispatched letters of contract to the kings of Cambria and of Cornwall: Our hand and seal will justify no less. So then do not so dishonor me, my lords, as to make a shipwreck of our kingly word.

"I am as kind as is the pelican that kills itself to save her young ones' lives."

The pelican was believed to wound its own breast in order to feed its young with its blood.

He continued, "And yet I am as jealous as the princely eagle that kills her young ones if they do but look with dazzled eyes upon the radiant splendor of the sun."

Eagles were thought to be able to look directly at the sun. According to folklore, parent eagles tested their young eagles to see if they had this ability. If the young eagle's eyes watered while looking at the sun, the young eagle was killed.

King Leir continued, "Within the next two days, I expect the coming of the King of Cornwall and the King of Cambria."

At that moment, the two kings walked into the room.

Seeing them, King Leir said, "But at a good and opportune time, they have arrived already."

He then said to the two kings, "This haste of yours, my lords, testifies to the fervent love you bear my daughters. Think yourselves as welcome to King Leir as Priam's children ever were to him."

King Priam of Troy had fifty sons and many daughters. He greatly mourned when Achilles, the greatest warrior of the Trojan War, killed his — Priam's — oldest son, Hector.

The King of Cornwall said, "My gracious lord, and father-in-law, too, I hope, pardon me for not making greater haste, but if my horse were as swift as is my will, I long before this time would have seen your majesty."

The King of Cambria said, "No other excuse of absence can I frame than what my brother has informed your grace. In return for our undeserved welcome, we vow perpetually to rest at your command."

The King of Cornwall said, "But you, sweet love, illustrious Gonorill, who is the regent and the sovereign of my soul, am I, the King of Cornwall, welcome to you, your excellency?"

Gonorill replied, "You are as welcome as Leander was to Hero, or as brave Aeneas was to the Carthaginian queen, so and more welcome is your grace to me."

She had referred to two ancient love stories that had ended badly. Leander loved Hero, and he swam across the Hellespont each night to see her. One night he drowned, and Hero then committed suicide.

After the Greeks sacked the city of Troy, the Trojan Aeneas went to Carthage and had an affair with its queen: Dido. But Aeneas' destiny was to go to Italy, and after he left her, she committed suicide.

The King of Cambria, whose name was Morgan, said, "Oh, may my fortune prove no worse than the King of Cornwall's since the Heavens know my fancy is as much. Dear Ragan, say whether I am welcome to you. All welcomes other than yours will little comfort me."

Ragan replied, "As gold is welcome to the covetous eye, as sleep is welcome to the traveler, as fresh water is welcome to sea-beaten men, or moistened showers are welcome to the parched ground, or anything more welcome than these things I have mentioned, so and more welcome lovely Morgan is."

King Leir said, "What remains, then, but that we consummate the celebration of these wedding rites? My kingdom I equally divide. Princes, draw lots, and take your chance."

The two kings drew lots.

King Leir continued, "These I resign as freely unto you as formerly by true succession they were mine. And here I freely dispossess myself of my kingdom and make you two my true adopted heirs.

"I myself will sojourn with my son-in-law of Cornwall and take me to my prayers and my prayer-beads. I know my daughter Ragan will be sorry because I do not spend my days with her.

"I wish I were able to be with both of my daughters at once: They are the kindest girls in Christendom."

Perillus said, "I have been silent all this while, my lord, to see if anyone worthier than myself would once have spoken up for poor Cordella, but either love or fear ties silence to their tongues. Oh, hear me speak for her, my gracious lord. Her deeds have not deserved this ruthless judgment, which has disinherited her of everything."

King Leir said, "Urge this no more if you love your life! I say any woman is no daughter if she scorns to tell her father how she loves him. Whoever speaks to me about this again, I will regard him as my mortal foe.

"Come, let us go in to celebrate with joy the happy nuptials of these two loving pairs."

Everyone except Perillus exited.

Perillus said to himself, "Ah, who is so blind as those who will not see the close approach of their own misery?

"Poor lady, I extremely pity her, and while I live, each drop of my heart's blood will I squeeze out in order to do her any good I can."

— 2.4 —

— Scene 7 —

The King of Gallia and Mumford, disguised as religious pilgrims, talked together.

Mumford said, "My lord, how do you like this British air?"

Upset because Mumford was forgetting that they were in disguise as pilgrims and so Mumford ought not to address him as "my lord," the King of Gallia said, "'My lord'? I warned you against this foolish habit of yours and bound you to the contrary, you know. Do not address me as your lord."

"Pardon me for once, my lord, I forgot," Mumford said.

King of Gallia said sarcastically, "'My lord' again? Then let's have nothing else but 'lord' and so be taken for spies, and then it is 'well.'"

"By God's wounds, I could bite my tongue in two out of anger at myself!" Mumford said. "For God's sake name yourself some proper name."

"Call me Tresillus," the King of Gallia said. "I'll call you Denapoll."

These were quasi-pastoral names that the King of Gallia knew because of his excellent education.

"Even if I might be made the monarch of the world, I could not hit upon these names, I swear," Mumford said.

"Then call me Will," the King of Gallia said. "I'll call you Jack."

"Well, so be it," Mumford replied, "for I have well deserved to be called Jack."

A jack is a low-bred fellow; Mumford was criticizing himself for continually calling his disguised king "my lord."

Cordella arrived.

The disguised King of Gallia said to Mumford quietly, "Stand concealed, for here comes a British lady. A more beautiful creature my eyes have never beheld."

Unaware that she was not alone, Cordella said to herself, "This is a day of joy to my sisters, a day in which they both are married to kings, and I, by birth as worthy as themselves, am turned out into the world to seek my fortune.

"How may I blame the fickle Queen of Chance — Lady Fortune — who is making me an example of her power? Ah, I am a poor, weak maiden, whose weakness is very unable to endure these assaults of fortune! Oh, father Leir, how you wrong your child who was always obedient to your will!

"But why do I accuse Lady Fortune and my father? No, no, it is the pleasure of my God, and I willingly embrace the rod."

Proverbs 5 states, "*Foolishness is bound in the heart of a child: but the rod of correction shall drive it away from him*" (1599 Geneva Bible).

The disguised King of Gallia said, "She is no goddess, for she cries out against Lady Fortune and about the unkindness and unnaturalness of her father."

Her father, King Leir, was unnatural because he was not acting as a father naturally should. He was throwing her out of his palace.

"These costly robes, ill suitable for my now low estate," Cordella said, "I will exchange for other meaner clothing."

"If I had a kingdom in my hands," Mumford said, "I would exchange it for a milkmaid's smock and petticoat so that she and I might exchange our clothes together."

This would be a way for him to see Cordella naked — and for him to be naked with her.

Cordella said, "I will take myself to my thread and needle, and earn my living with my fingers' ends. I will be a seamstress to earn my bread."

"Oh, splendid!" Mumford said. "God willing, you shall have my custom, I seriously swear by sweet St. Denis, for all the shirts and night clothing that I wear!"

St. Denis is the patron saint of France.

"I will profess and vow to live a maiden's life," Cordella said.

"Then I protest that you shall not have my custom," Mumford said.

He did not want her to live the life of a maiden — a virgin.

The King of Gallia said, "I can refrain no longer from speaking, for if I do I think my heart will be breaking."

"By God's blood," Mumford said, "Will, I hope you are not in love with my seamstress!"

The disguised King of Gallia said, "I am in such a labyrinth of love that I don't know which way to take to get out."

Mumford replied, "You'll never get out unless you first get in."

Mumford being Mumford, when he said "get in," he was probably thinking of Cordella's vagina.

"Please, Jack," the disguised King of Gallia said, "don't oppose my passions."

"Please, Will," Mumford said, "go to her and test her patience. See what she will think of you."

The disguised King of Gallia and Mumford came out of concealment.

The disguised King of Gallia said to Cordella, "Whoever you are, you fairest creature whom any mortal eyes ever beheld, I, who have overheard your woes, ask you to reveal to me the cause of these your sad laments."

"Ah, pilgrims," Cordella said, "what good is it to show the cause when there's no means to find a remedy?"

The disguised King of Gallia replied, "To talk about grief eases a heart overburdened with grief."

"To touch a sore aggravates the pain," Cordella said.

"The weak mouse, by virtue of her teeth, released the princely lion from the net," the disguised King of Gallia said.

He was referring to one of Aesop's fables: A lion once caught a mouse, which begged for its life and promised to reward the lion for its mercy. The lion laughed at the mouse but released it. Later, the lion was trapped in a rope trap. It roared, and the mouse heard the lion's roars, came, and gnawed the ropes until the lion was free.

"Kind palmer, who so much desires to hear the tragic tale of my unhappy youth," Cordella said, "know this in brief: I am the luckless daughter of Leir, formerly King of Britain."

"Why," the disguised King of Gallia said, "who prevents his honorable age — Leir — from being still the King of Britain?"

"No one but himself has dispossessed himself," Cordella said. "He has given all his kingdom to the kings of Cornwall and Cambria along with my sisters in marriage."

"Has he given nothing to your lovely self?" the King of Gallia asked.

"He didn't love me and therefore he gave me nothing, only because I could not flatter him," Cordella said, "and in this day of triumph to my sisters Lady Fortune triumphs in my overthrow."

"Sweet lady, suppose that there should come a king — as good as either of your sisters' husbands — to ask you for your love: Would you accept him?"

"Oh, do not mock those in misery," Cordella replied, "and do not think that even though Lady Fortune has the power to spoil my honor and debase my state, she has any effect on my mind, for if the greatest monarch on the earth should plead his love to me in this extremity, unless my heart could love and my heart could like him better than any man I ever saw, his great estate no more should move my mind than mountains move by blast of every wind."

"Don't think, sweet nymph," the disguised King of Gallia said, "that it is a holy palmer's practice to devise fresh torments for grieved souls; therefore, in witness of my true intent, let Heaven and Earth bear record of my words: There is a young and robust King of Gallia, who resembles me as much as I resemble myself, who earnestly begs to have your love and join with you in Hymen's sacred bonds. He wants to marry you."

Cordella thought, *The like to you did never these eyes of mine behold. I have never seen anyone as handsome as you. Oh, live to add new torments to my grief! Why did you thus entrap me in love unawares?*

She said out loud, "Ah, palmer, my estate is not fitting for a kingly marriage as the case now stands. Once when I lived in honor's height, a prince perhaps might request my love. But now misery, dishonor, and disgrace has fallen on me, and quite reversed the case.

"Your king will consider you wise if you cease the suit where no dowry will ensue. So then be advised, palmer, what to do: Cease seeking a wife for your king; instead, seek a wife for yourself to woo."

The disguised King of Gallia said, "Your birth's too high for any but a king to wed you."

"My mind is low — that is, modest and humble — enough to love a palmer rather than any king upon the Earth," Cordella replied.

"Oh, but you never can endure their life," the disguised King of Gallia said, "which is so strictly moral and full of poverty."

"Oh, yes, I can, and I would be happy if I might," Cordella said. "I'll hold your palmer's staff within my hand and think it is the scepter of a queen. Sometimes I'll set your hat on my head and think that I am wearing a rich imperial crown. Sometimes I'll help you in your holy prayers and think I am with you in Paradise. Thus I'll mock Fortune as she mocks me, and never will I repent my lovely choice, for by having you, I shall have all content."

The disguised King of Gallia thought, *It would be a sin to hold her longer in suspense since my soul has vowed she shall be mine.*

He said out loud, "Ah, dear Cordella, cordial to my heart, I am no palmer as I seem to be, for I have come hither in this unknown disguise to view the admired beauty of those eyes."

He was punning on the word "Cordella" — a cordial is a refreshing, invigorating drink.

He continued, "I am the King of Gallia, gentle maiden, although I am accompanied by few attendants, as you can see, and yet I am your vassal due to imperious Love, and I am now sworn to serve you everlastingly."

The King of Gallia took off his palmer's disguise.

"Whoever you are, whether of high or low descent, all's one to me," Cordella said. "I request only this: That as I am, you will accept me, and I will have you as whosoever you are. Yet well I know you come of royal race: I see such sparks of honor in your face."

"Have palmers' clothes such power to win fair ladies?" Mumford said. "By my faith, then I hope the next lady who falls is mine."

"Falls" may mean "falls in love," but Mumford being Mumford, it may mean "falls in bed."

He continued, "Upon condition I might fare no worse than the king, I would forever wear a palmer's clothing. I like an honest and plain-dealing wench who swears, without exceptions, 'I will have you.'

"These foppets — fools! — who don't know whether to love a man or not — unless they first go and ask their mothers' permission — by this hand, I hate them ten times worse than poison."

"What remains," the King of Gallia said, "for us to do to procure our happiness?"

"Indeed," Mumford said, "you must go to church to make the matter sure."

"It shall be so because the world shall say, 'King Leir's three daughters were wedded in one day,'" the King of Gallia said. "The celebration of this happy chance we will defer until we come to France."

"I like the wooing that's not long in doing," Mumford said.

One meaning of "to do" is "to have sex."

He continued, "Well, for her sake, I know what I know: I'll never marry while I live unless I have one of these British ladies. My disposition is alienated from the maidens of France. I will no longer love French ladies. "

CHAPTER 3

— 3.1 —

— Scene 8 —

Alone, Perillus said to himself, "The king has dispossessed himself of all he had in order to advance those who scarcely will give him thanks. He has turned away his youngest daughter, and no man knows what has become of her. He sojourns now in Cornwall with his eldest daughter, Gonorill, who flattered him until she obtained from his hands the wealth that she now possesses, and now that she sees he has no more to give, it grieves her heart to see her father live.

"Oh, whom should man trust in this wicked age when children thus rage against their parents? But he, the model of mild Christian patience, puts up with all wrongs and never gives reply, yet she is not ashamed to call him 'fool' and 'senile dotard' to his face in the most vituperative way, and she commands her parasitic hangers-on to carry out her orders to often contemptuously scoff at and offer him disgrace.

"Oh, iron age! Oh, the times! Oh, monstrous, vile, when parents are condemned by the child! His pension she has half taken away from him, and she will, before long, take the other half, I fear, for she thinks nothing is bestowed in vain except that which maintains her father's life. Trust not friends or relatives, but trust strangers instead, since daughters prove disloyal to the father."

In his *First Oration Against Catiline*, Cicero wrote, "*O tempora o mores*," which means, "Oh, the times! Oh, the behavior!" He was lamenting times and behavior that could produce such a monster as Catiline, who wished to overthrow the Roman Republic.

Perillus continued, "Well, I will advise him the best I can. I wish that I were able to redress and correct this wrong! Yet he shall be sure I will do what I can do to my utmost power to the final hour — his hour of death."

— 3.2 —

31

— Scene 9 —

Gonorill and Skalliger talked together.

Using the regal plural, Gonorill said, "I request, Skalliger, that you tell me what you think. Could any woman of our high rank endure such imperious comments and peremptory taunts as I do daily from my doting father?"

The word "doting" means 1) foolish affection or 2) senile stupidity, or 3) both.

She continued, "Doesn't it suffice that out of charity I keep him, a man who is not able to keep himself, yet he should think to reprimand me and snap at me with every word as if he were our better?

"I cannot make myself a new-fashioned gown, and set it forth with more than common cost, but his old, doting, doltish, foolish, withered wit is sure to give me a senseless, unnecessary rebuke for it.

"I cannot make a banquet extraordinary to grace myself and spread my name abroad but he, the old fool, is captious and eager to find fault by and by, and says that the cost would well suffice for two banquets.

"Judge then, please, what reason is it that I should stand alone charged with his vain expense and that my sister Ragan should go free, to whom he gave as much as he gave to me?

"I ask you, Skalliger, to tell me, if you know, by any means I can rid myself of this woe."

"Your many favors continually bestowed on me bind me in duty to advise your grace how you may soonest remedy this ill," Skalliger replied. "The large allowance that he has from you is that which makes him so forget himself and his place. Therefore, reduce his allowance by half and you shall see that, having less, he will be more thankful for what he has, because abundance makes us forget the fountains from whence the benefits spring."

"Well, Skalliger, for your kind advice herein, I will not be ungrateful if I live," Gonorill said. "I have taken away half his portion already, and I will immediately take away the other half, so that, having no means to relieve himself, he may go seek elsewhere for better help."

Gonorill exited.

Alone, Skalliger said to himself, "Go, viperous woman, shame to all your sex, the Heavens no doubt will punish you for this, and the Heavens will punish me, a villain who, to curry favor, have given the daughter advice that is against the father."

Exodus 20:12 states, "*Honour thy father and thy mother: that thy days may be long upon the land which the Lord thy God giveth thee*" (King James Version).

People in this culture thought that vipers birthed themselves by biting their way out of their mother.

He added, "But to us the world this experience does give: He who cannot flatter cannot live."

— 3.3 —

— Scene 10 —

The King of Cornwall, Leir, Perillus, and some nobles stood together. The King of Cornwall was now married to Leir's oldest daughter, Gonorill.

The King of Cornwall asked Leir, "Father-in-law, why are you so sad? I think that you don't enjoy yourself as you used to do."

"The nearer we grow to our graves," Leir said, "the less we delight in worldly joys."

"But if a man can open himself to mirth," the King of Cornwall said, "it is a means by which to prolong his life."

Leir replied, "Then I welcome sorrow, Leir's only friend, who desires his troubled days to come to an end."

Seeing Gonorill coming, the King of Cornwall said, "Comfort yourself, father-in-law, here comes your daughter, who much will grieve, I know, to see you sad."

Gonorill walked over to them.

"But she grieves more, I fear, to see me live," Leir said.

The King of Cornwall said, "My Gonorill, you come at a wished-for time to take your father out of these pensive low spirits. Truly, I fear that all things do not go well."

"What, do you fear that I have angered him?" Gonorill replied. "Has he complained about me to my lord and husband? I'll provide him with a piece of bread and cheese — peasants' food — for soon he'll scheme nothing else than to carry false tales from one person to another. All his scheming is for the purpose of kindling strife between you, my lord and husband, and me, your loving wife.

"But I will make arrangements, if I can, to stop the effect where first the cause began. The cause began with Leir, and I will stop the effect by stopping Leir."

"Sweetheart, don't be angry in a biased cause," the King of Cornwall replied. "Leir has never complained about you in all his life."

He then said to Leir, "Father-in-law, you must not take seriously a woman's words."

"Alas, not I," Leir said. "Poor soul, she breeds young bones, and that is surely what makes her so touchy."

"Young bones" can mean 1) "new bones of contention," and/or "young bones of a fetus."

"What, 'breeds young bones' — already!" Gonorill said. "You will make an 'honest' and 'chaste' woman of me then, perhaps."

She objected to being thought pregnant so soon after her wedding.

Gonorill continued, "Oh, vile old wretch! Whoever heard the like? Whoever heard of a father seeking like this to defame his own child?"

The King of Cornwall said, "I cannot stay to hear this discordant sound."

He exited.

Gonorill said to Leir, her father, and to his attendants, "As for anyone who loves your company, you may go pack and seek some other place to sow the seed of discord and disgrace."

She exited.

Leir said, "As you can see, even if I say or do the best that ever I can, whatever I say or do is wrested and twisted immediately into another sense that makes it seem as if I am an evil old man. This punishment my heavy sins deserve, and more than this ten thousand thousand times, or else aged Leir could never find being cruel to him those people to whom he has been kind.

"Why do I live too long to see the course of nature quite reversed in my case? Gonorill, who came from me, is behaving unnaturally to me: It is unnatural for a daughter to treat a father the way she treats me.

"Ah, gentle Death, if ever any human being wished for your presence with a perfect zeal, then come to me, I beg you, even with all my heart, and end my sorrows with your fatal dart."

A dart is a spear or an arrow.

He wept.

"Ah, do not so distress yourself and make yourself despair without consolation," Perillus said, "nor dew your aged cheeks with strength-wasting tears."

Leir asked, "What man are you who takes any pity upon the worthless state of old Leir?"

"I am a man who bears as great a share of grief," Perillus said, "as if you were my dearest father and he was in this situation."

"Ah, my good friend," Leir said, "how ill are you advised to consort with impoverished miserable men. It simply is not intelligent to help poor men when you can consort with wealthy men. Go learn to flatter where you may in time get favor among the mighty, and so climb. For now I am so poor and full of need that I can never recompense your love."

"What's gotten by flattery does not long endure," Perillus said, "and men in favor do not live most secure. My conscience tells me that if I should forsake and abandon you, I would be the most hateful excrement on the earth. I do well know, in the course of former times, how good you, my lord, have been to me and mine."

"Did I ever raise you higher than the rest of all your ancestors who were before you?" Leir asked.

"I never did seek that," Perillus said, "but by your good grace I always enjoyed my own rank with quietness."

"Did I ever give you additional income to increase the income rightfully given to you by your father when he died?"

"I had enough, my lord," Perillus said, "and having that, why should you need to give me any more?"

"Oh, did I ever dispossess myself and give you half my kingdom out of my good will?" Leir asked.

"Alas, my lord," Perillus said, "there was no reason why you should have such a thought to give it to me."

He said "alas" because he disliked his king asking him that question, not because he mourned not having half the kingdom.

"If you talk of reason, then be mute," Leir said, "for with good reason I can refute you and prove you wrong. If they, who first by nature's sacred law owe to me the tribute of their lives, if they to whom I always have been kind and bountiful beyond comparison, if they for whom I have ruined myself and brought my age to this extreme need, do now reject, condemn, despise, and abhor me, what reason moves you to sorrow for me?"

Leir had given his daughter Gonorill life and had treated her well, and so by the law of nature — a law that is implanted in human minds by nature and that can be known by reason — Gonorill owed him respect and love.

"Where reason fails, let tears confirm my love, and speak how much your passions move me," Perillus said. "Ah, my good lord, don't condemn all daughters because of the actions of one daughter. You have two daughters left to whom I know you shall be welcome, if you please to go and see them."

"Oh, how your words add sorrow to my soul, because they make me think of my unkindness to Cordella, whom without cause and reason I dispossessed of everything upon hearing the unkind suggestions of her sisters. I did not treat her the way a father ought to. And for her sake I think this heavy doom has fallen on me, and not without desert: I deserve this because of the way I treated Cordella.

"Yet I was always kind to Ragan, and I gave to her half of all I had. It may be, if I should go to her, she would be kinder to me than Gonorill and would treat me fairly and well."

"No doubt she would," Perillus said, "and she would plan, before much longer, to redress your wrong by force of arms."

"Well, since you advise me to go to Ragan," Leir said, "I am resolved to try the worst of woe."

"To try" means "to test." Leir was still discouraged, and he was going to test whether things would get worse if he visited his daughter Ragan.

— 3.4 —

— Scene 11 —

Alone, Ragan talked to herself.

"How may I bless the hour of my birth that foretold to me that I would have such happy astrological stars! How may I thank kind Fortune that promises to all my actions such a desired outcome!

"I rule my husband, the King of Cambria, as I please; the members of the body politic — the nobles, clergy, and common people — are all obedient to my will and see to it that whatever I say shall be done. No one dares to answer no to anything I say.

"My eldest sister lives in royal state and lacks nothing fitting her degree. Yet she has such a cooling card — my father — who dampens her enthusiasm for her life so much that her honey tastes much like gall.

"My father, Leir, with her is quartermaster still, and many times restrains her and her will — he tells her no — but, if he were with me, and treated me like that, I'd send him packing to go somewhere else. I'd entertain him with such slender cost that he should quickly wish to change his host."

— Scene 12 —

The King of Cornwall and Gonorill talked. Some attendants were in the room.

"Ah, Gonorill," the King of Cornwall said, "what dire unhappy chance has separated your father from our presence in such a way that no report can yet be heard about him?

"Some great unkindness has been done to him, far exceeding the bounds of patience; otherwise, all the world shall never persuade me that he would forsake us without notice."

"Alas, my lord, whom does it touch so near, or who has interest in this grief but I, whom sorrow would have brought to her longest home — the grave — except that I know his character so well?

"I know that he has only stolen upon my sister without notice to see how she fares and spend a little time with her in order to see how all things go and how she likes her choice of husband, and when occasion serves, he'll steal from her and without notice return to us again.

"Therefore, my lord, be frolicsome and know that you will see my father here again before long."

"I hope so, too," the King of Cornwall said, "but still to be surer I'll send a post immediately to know whether he has arrived there."

He exited with his attendants.

Alone, Gonorill said to herself, "But I will intercept the messenger and work upon and mold him, before he departs, with sweet persuasions and with sound rewards and remuneration, so that his report shall confirm my speech and make my lord and husband cease further to inquire. I will make sure that the messenger reports what I want him to report.

"If my father, Leir, has not gone to my sister's court, as my mind tells me that he surely has, he perhaps may, by travelling unknown ways, have fallen sick and be dead and have been buried as a common traveler.

"I wish to God that my fortune were so good as that, for then there would be no more to do but to say this: 'He went away, and no one knows where he is.'

"But let's say that he is in Cambria with its king and there he exclaims against me, as he will. I know he is as welcome to my sister as water is welcome inside a broken ship.

"Well, after him I'll send such thunderclaps of slander, scandal, and invented tales that all the blame shall be removed from me and, unperceived, rebound upon himself.

"Thus with one nail another I'll expel, and make the world judge that I treated him well."

The messenger who would go to Cambria arrived, carrying a letter in his hand.

"My honest friend," Gonorill asked, "where are you going away so fast?"

"To Cambria, madam, with a letter from the king your husband," the messenger answered.

"A letter to whom?" Gonorill asked.

"To your father, if he is there," the messenger answered.

"Let me see the letter," Gonorill ordered.

She grabbed and opened the letter.

"Madam, I hope your grace will stand between me and my neck-verse if I be called in question for opening the king's letter," the shocked messenger said.

In this society, a person could escape being hung if he could prove that he could read Latin. In such a case, the person would be tried in an ecclesiastical court — only priests and other religious could read Latin. Ecclesiastical courts were often more lenient than secular courts. The verse to be read in Latin was often called the neck-verse because it could save someone's neck.

Often the neck-verse was Psalm 51:1 (1599 Geneva Bible):

To him that excelleth. A Psalm of David, when the Prophet Nathan came unto him, after he had gone in to Bathsheba.

1 "Have mercy upon me, O God, according to thy loving-kindness: according to the multitude of thy compassions put away mine iniquities."

Here is the original Latin from *Psalmus* 50 (51) (Vulgate Bible):

1 In finem Psalmus David

2. Cum venit ad eum Nathan propheta quando intravit ad Bethsabee

3. Miserere mei Deus secundum magnam misericordiam tuam et secundum multitudinem miserationum tuarum dele iniquitatem meam

Note that different Bibles follow different numbering systems for the Psalms.

"It was I who opened the letter," Gonorill said. "It was not you."

"Yes, but you need not care, but I, a handsome man, must be quickly tied up; and when a man's hanged, all the world cannot save him."

"He who hangs you would do better to hang his father," Gonorill said. "That is true of anyone who hurts you in the least degree."

Using the royal plural, she added, "I tell you that we make great account of you. We regard you highly."

"I am overjoyed," the messenger said. "I feast on your sweet words. Kind queen, if I had a hundred lives, I would spend ninety-nine of them for you on account of that kind word."

"Yes, but you would keep one life still," Gonorill said, "and that's as many as you are likely to have."

"That one life is not too dear for my good queen," the messenger said. "This sword, this shield, this head, this heart, these hands, arms, legs, guts, bowels, and all the members else whatsoever, are at your disposal. Use me, trust me, command me; if I fail in anything, tie me to a dung cart and make a scavenger's horse of me, and whip me as long as I have any skin on my back."

A scavenger was a street-cleaner.

"In token of further employment, take that," Gonorill said, giving him money.

"A strong bond, a firm obligation, good in law, good in law," the messenger said. "If I don't keep the condition, let my neck be the forfeiture of my negligence. If I don't do what you tell me to do, then hang me."

"I like you well," Gonorill said. "You have a good tongue in your head. You say the right things."

"And I have as bad a tongue, if it is set on being bad, as any oyster-wife at the fish market in Billingsgate has," the messenger said. "Why, I have made many of my neighbors forsake their houses and go dwell elsewhere by complaining about and criticizing them, and so, by my means, houses have been quite cheap in our parish. My tongue being well whetted and honed with anger is sharper than a high-quality razor of Palermo."

"Oh, you are a fit man for my purpose," Gonorill said.

"Don't praise me, sweet queen, before you test me," the messenger said. "As my deserts are, so think of me. If I give you good results, then praise me."

"Well said," Gonorill replied. "This then is your trial: Instead of carrying the king's letter to my father, carry this letter to my sister, which contains content quite contrary to the other. By means of my letter, she shall be given to understand that my father has defamed her, has given out slanderous speeches against her, and has most intolerably abused me, set my lord and me to arguing, and made mutinies among the commoners.

"These things — although they are not true — yet you must affirm them to be true with such oaths and protestations as will serve to drive my sister out of love with him and cause what I want to be accomplished.

"This done, you have won my favor forever, and you make a highway of preferment to you and all your friends. Do this, and good things will happen to you and to all your friends."

"That is sufficient," the messenger said. "Consider that it is already done — because it will be done. I will so tongue-whip Leir that I will leave him as bare of credit as a poulterer leaves a cony when she pulls off the rabbit's skin."

"Yet there is a further matter," Gonorill said.

"I am eager to hear what it is," the messenger said.

"If my sister thinks it convenient, as my letter will advocate, to make away with him and kill him, have you the heart to do it? Are you willing to murder my father?"

"Few words are best in so small a matter," the messenger said. "These are but trifles. By this book I swear I will."

He kissed the letter.

A person who took an oath in a law court kissed the Bible.

"Go about your errand immediately," Gonorill said. "I am eager for it to be done."

The messenger said as he exited, "I fly, I fly."

CHAPTER 4

— Scene 13 —

Alone, outside a church in Gallia, Cordella said to herself, "I have been too negligent today about going to the temple of my God to render thanks for all of His benefits that He miraculously has bestowed on me in raising me out of my mean estate when I was devoid of worldly friends and placing me in such a sweet state of happiness that far exceeds the reach of my merits.

"My kingly husband, the model of his time for zeal, for justice, for kindness, and for his care and concern for God, his subjects, me, and the common welfare, by God's appointment was ordained for me.

"I cannot wish for anything that I need or lack, but I may have it. Everything I want, I get. Almost.

"I have everything that I want, save for only this that I shall never obtain: my father's love.

"Oh, this I never shall gain. I would abstain from any nutriment and starve my body to the very bones. Barefoot, I would set forth unto the furthest quarters of the Earth on pilgrimage, and all my lifetime I would wear sackcloth, and like a mourner I would pour dust upon my head, as long as he would please to forgive me one day, so that his grey hairs might go to Heaven in peace.

"And yet I don't know how I offended him, or in what I have justly deserved blame.

"Oh, sisters! You are much to blame in this. It was not he but you who did me wrong. Yet may God forgive both him and you and me, even as I do in perfect Christian love and charity.

"I will go to church now and pray to my Savior and ask that, before I die, I may obtain my father's favor."

— 4.2 —

— Scene 14 —

Leir and Perillus were faint and suffering and weak. Both of them were old.

Perillus said to Leir, "Rest on me, my lord, and support yourself. The way seems long and tiresome to your aged limbs."

"No, rest on me, kind friend, and support yourself," Leir replied. "You are as old as I am, but kinder."

"Ah, my good lord," Perillus said, "it is not fitting that I should lean upon the person of a king."

"But it is worse fitting that I should bring you forth with me," Leir said. "You had no cause to come along with me, through these unfamiliar paths and exhausting ways, and never ease your fainting limbs a whit. You have left all — yes, all — to come with me, and I, for the all you have left behind, have nothing to reward you with."

"Cease, my good lord," Perillus replied, "to aggravate my woes with these kind words, which cut my heart in two when I think that your will should lack the power to do what it wants."

"Cease, good Perillus," Leir said, "to call me 'lord,' and think that I am only the shadow of myself."

"That honorable title of 'lord' I will give to my lord as long as I live," Perillus said. "Oh, be of comfort, for I see the place where your daughter keeps her residence. And, look, in happy time the Cambrian prince has arrived here to welcome our coming."

The King of Cambria, Ragan, and some nobles walked over to them, looked at them, and then whispered together.

"Would it be better for me to speak or to sit down and die?" Leir asked. "I am ashamed to tell this heavy tale."

"Then let me tell it, if you please, my lord," Perillus said. "It is a shame for them who were the cause of the situation you are in."

"What two old men are those who seem so sad?" the King of Cambria asked, "I think I should remember well their looks."

"I am not mistaken," Ragan said. "Surely he is my father."

She thought, *I must pretend to be kind now of necessity.*

Ragan ran to Leir, and knelt before him, saying, "Father, I bid you welcome, full of grief, to see your grace treated thus unworthily. It is ill-befitting your reverend old age for you to come on foot a journey so unendurable.

"Oh, what disastrous event has been the cause to make your cheeks so hollow, spare, and lean?"

She said to the others with her, "He cannot speak for weeping. For God's love, come, let us refresh him with some needful things and at more leisure we may better know from whence springs the ground of this unlooked-for woe."

"Come, father-in-law," the King of Cambria said. "Before we talk any further, you shall refresh yourself after this weary walk."

Everyone except Ragan exited.

Alone, she said to herself, "Has he come to me with his finger in his eye to tell a tale against my sister here, whom I know he greatly has abused?"

If you ever need to cry without a good reason, put your finger in your eye.

She continued, "And now, like a contentious crafty wretch, he himself first begins to complain, when actually he himself is in the greatest fault. I'll not be partial in my sister's cause, nor yet believe the reports of his foolish old age. He, for a trifling reason, I dare safely say, has stolen away from my sister because of a sudden, angry impulse, and here, indeed, he hopes to have harbor and to be cooed to and fussed over like a child.

"But before long, his coming he shall curse, and truly say he came from bad to worse. Yet for a while I will make fair weather in order to procure a convenient reason to be angry at him, and then I'll strike it home."

— 4.3 —

— Scene 15 —

Alone, the messenger said to himself, "Now happily I have arrived here before the stately palace of the Cambrian king. If Leir is here safely seated and at rest, to rouse him from it I will do my best."

Ragan walked over to him.

The messenger said to himself, "Now, bags of gold, your virtue is, no doubt, to make me in my message bold and stout."

At the time, the word "stout" meant "brave."

He then said to Ragan, "May the King of Heaven preserve your majesty, and send your highness everlasting reign."

"Thanks, my good friend," Ragan said, "but what is your message?"

"Kind greetings from the Cornwall queen," the messenger said. "The rest of the message this letter will declare."

He handed Ragan the letter.

As she opened it, she asked, "How fares our royal sister?"

"I left her in good health when I departed," the messenger said.

Ragan read the letter, frowned, and stamped her foot.

Looking at her, the messenger thought, *See how her color comes and goes again: now as red as scarlet, now as pale as ash. See how she knits her brow, and bites her lips, and stamps her foot, and makes a dumbshow of disdain mixed with revenge and violent extremes.*

Some plays at the time included dumbshows, in which actors acted without dialogue.

The messenger thought, *Here will be more work and more crowns for me.*

The crowns he meant were coins with the image of a crown stamped on them.

Ragan said to herself about Leir and her sister, "Alas, poor soul, and has he treated her thus? And has he now come hither with intent to set a divorce between my husband and me?

"Does he proclaim that he has heard a report that I rule my husband as I wish, and therefore he means to alter that fact so that I shall know my lord to be my head?"

Ephesians 5:22-25 (1599 Geneva Bible) states this:

22 Wives, submit yourselves unto your husbands, as unto the Lord.

23 For the husband is the wife's head, even as Christ is the head of the Church, and the same is the Savior of his body.

24 Therefore as the Church is in subjection to Christ, even so let the wives be to their husbands in everything.

25 Husbands, love your wives, even as Christ loved the Church, and gave himself for it,

Ragan continued, "Well, it would be best for him to take good heed, or I will make him hop without a head for his presumption, dotard that he is."

She meant that she would behead her father.

She continued, "In Cornwall he has made such mutinies — first, setting the king against the queen, then stirring up the commoners against the king — that had he there continued any longer, he would have been investigated for his crimes, so for that reason he fled from there, and now he comes thus slyly stealing unto us, and now already since his coming here, my husband and he are grown in such a league that I can have no conference with my husband.

"I fear that my father already intimates some false and petty objections against my position in this state. It is therefore best to cut him off before he spreads slanderous rumors abroad, lest it becomes too late to reverse those rumors."

Ragan then said to the messenger, "Friend, as the tenor of these letters shows, my sister Gonorill puts great confidence in you."

"She has never yet committed any trust to me except that trust to which, I hope, she has always found me faithful," the messenger said. "Trustworthy will I be to any friend of hers who has occasion to employ my help."

"Do you have the heart to perform a stratagem, and give a stab or two if need should require them?" Ragan asked.

She wanted the messenger to murder her father.

"I have a heart packed tightly with adamant, the hardest rock known to man," the messenger said. "My heart and adamant have never known what melting pity meant. I regard no more the murdering of a man than I regard the squishing of a flea when I catch one biting on my skin.

"If you will have your husband or your father or both of them sent to another world, just command me to do it: It shall be done."

"What you have said is enough," Ragan said.

Using the royal plural, she added, "We have no doubts about you: You will do what you say you will do. Meet us tomorrow, here, at nine o'clock."

She gave him some money and said, "Meanwhile, farewell, and drink that for me."

She exited.

Alone, the messenger said to himself, "Yes, this money is what will make me do the deed. Oh, if I had such customers as her everyday, this would be the most profitable trade in Christendom! A bag of gold given in return for a paltry stab! Why, here's a wench who longs to have a sexual stab. Well, I could give it to her, and never hurt her neither."

— 4.4 —

— Scene 16 —

The King of Gallia and his now wife, Cordella, talked together.

He said, "When will these clouds of sorrow finally disperse and smiling joy triumph upon your brow? When will this scene of sadness have an end and pleasant acts ensue to move delight? When will my lovely queen cease to lament and take some comfort to her grieved thoughts? If of yourself you will not have any care, yet pity me whom your grief makes despair."

"Oh, don't grieve, my lord and husband," Cordella said. "You have no reason to grieve. Don't let my strong emotions move your mind even a small amount, for I am bound by nature to lament because of the ill will of him — my father — who first lent life to me. If the stalk is dried

48

up with disdain, withered and sere the branch must necessarily remain. Because my father disdains me, I must necessarily be sad."

"But you are now grafted to another stock," the King of Gallia said, punning on "stalk."

A branch can be grafted onto another tree, and the two become one. Similarly, a husband and wife become one.

He continued, "I am the stock and you are the lovely branch, and from my root continual sap shall flow to make you flourish with perpetual spring."

As a newlywed, he wanted to be happy and sexually satisfied, and he wanted his young wife to be happy and sexually satisfied. He wanted his "root" to continually flow with the sap of semen. Spring is a good time for babies to be born because they have time to grow before the hardships of winter; that is why we have so many weddings in June in the Northern hemisphere.

The King of Gallia continued, "Forget your father and your kindred now, since like inhuman and inhumane beasts they forsake you. Think that they are dead since all their kindness dies, and bury them where black oblivion lies.

"Don't think that you are the daughter of old Leir, who did unkindly — and not like a father — disinherit you; instead, think that you are the noble Gallian queen, and wife to him — me — who dearly loves you. Embrace the joys that here and now with you dwell. Let sorrow go packing and hide herself in hell."

Cordella replied, "That I miss my country or my kindred, my old acquaintance or my old friends does not by any means make my mind disordered — because I know you, who are dearer to me than country, kindred, and all things else can be.

"Yet pardon me, my gracious lord, in this, for what can stop the course of nature's power?

"As easy is it for four-footed beasts to suspend themselves upon the liquid air and mount aloft into the element and outstrip the feathered fowls in flight,

"As easy is it for the slimy fish to live and thrive without the help of water,

"As easy is it for a black person to wash the black color from his skin,

"All of which things oppose the course of nature,

"As easy as those things am I able to forget my father."

"Mirror of virtue, and Phoenix of our age!" the King of Gallia said. "You are too kind a daughter for such an unkind father!"

A mirror of virtue is a model of virtue.

The Phoenix is a mythological bird symbolizing rebirth and resurrection. Every few hundred years, the Phoenix sets itself on fire and then is reborn from the flames. The King of Gallia was referring to Cordella as a symbol of virtue that will never die out although at times many people — such as Leir and Cordella's sisters — exhibit a lack of virtue. As a symbol of new life arising from the ashes of the past, the Phoenix is a symbol of immortality.

In addition, Phoenix is a character in Homer's *Iliad*. He is a father-figure and a would-be peacemaker to Achilles, who treats him respectfully although he does not say the things that Phoenix wants him to say. (After Achilles grows angry at Agamemnon and refuses to fight in the Trojan War, an action that results in the Trojans being victorious in battle, Phoenix wants Achilles to agree to go back into battle and fight for Agamemnon. Achilles refuses.)

The King of Gallia continued, "Be of good comfort, for I will dispatch ambassadors immediately for Britain, to go to the King of Cornwall's court, where your father now is staying, and in the kindest manner my ambassadors will entreat him to set former grievances apart and be pleased to come and visit us.

"If no entreaty will accomplish that, I'll offer him half of all my crown and let him rule with me.

"If that does not move him to come here, we'll furnish a fleet and sail to Cornwall to visit him, and there you shall be firmly reconciled in perfect love, just as you used to be."

"Where tongue cannot sufficient thanks afford," Cordella said, "may the King of Heaven reward my lord."

"Just be blithe and frolic, sweetheart, with me," the King of Gallia said. "This and much more I'll do to comfort you."

— 4.5 —

— Scene 17 —

Alone, the messenger said to himself, "It is a marvel to see, now I am flush with money, how many friends I purchase everywhere! How many seek to creep into my favor, and kiss their hands and bend their knees to me to show me respect!"

Seeing Ragan coming, he said to himself, "No more, here comes the queen; now I shall know her mind, and I hope to gain more money from her."

Ragan walked over to him and said, "My friend, I see you remembered your promise well and are before me here, I think, today."

Obviously, the messenger had arrived before she had, but she did not like to give credit where credit was due.

"I am a poor man, if it please your grace," the messenger said, "but yet I always love to keep my word."

His politic answer avoided pointing out that he had arrived there first.

"Well, keep your word with me," Ragan said, "and you shall see that instead of your being a poor man I will make you rich."

"I long to hear your orders," the messenger said. "What you want might have already been dispatched if you had told me of it the previous night."

51

"Dispatched" meant "completed." What Ragan wanted to be completed was the dispatch — the murder — of her father. She wanted his life to be completed.

"It is a thing of very strange consequence," Ragan said, "and I cannot well utter it in words."

She was lying. It would not bother her to say in words that she wanted the messenger to kill her father.

"It is stranger that I am not by this beside myself with longing to hear it," the messenger said.

He was lying. He was beside himself with longing to hear her orders. Carrying out her orders would bring him money.

The messenger continued, "Even if your orders were to meet the devil in his den and try a bout with him for a scratched face, I'd undertake it if you would only tell me to."

"Ah, my good friend," Ragan said, "that which I would have you do is such a thing as I am ashamed to say, yet it needs to be done."

"I'll speak it for you, queen," the messenger said. "Shall I kill your father? I know that is what you want me to do. If that is so, tell me yes."

"Yes," Ragan said.

"Why, that's enough," the messenger said.

"And yet that is not all," Ragan said.

"What else?" the messenger asked.

"You must kill that old man — Perillus — who came with my father."

"Here are two hands," the messenger said, holding out his hands. "Each of my hands can make a man a corpse. I can kill both Leir and Perillus."

"And for each hand here is a recompense," Ragan said.

She gave him two bags of money.

"Oh, I wish that I had ten hands by a miracle," the messenger said. "I could tear ten people to pieces with my teeth so in my mouth you'd also put a purse of gold. But in what manner must it be effected?"

"Tomorrow morning before the break of day," Ragan said, "I by a stratagem will send them to the thicket that is about some two miles from the court, and I will promise to meet them there myself because I must have a private conference with them about some news I have received from the King of Cornwall.

"This is enough, I know. They will not fail to show up, so be ready to play your part then. Once the deed is done, you may very easily escape and no man will ever suspect you of committing the crime.

"But yet, before you prosecute the act, show my father the letter that my sister sent to me. In the letter let him read his own indictment first, and then proceed to execution.

"But see that you don't grow fainthearted, for they will speak fair words to you and try to persuade you not to kill them."

"Even if he could speak words as pleasing as the pipe of the god Mercury, who played music that charmed the hundred eyes of watchful Argos and made him fall asleep, yet here are words so pleasing to my thoughts" — the messenger jingled the coins in the moneybags — "as shall quite take away the sound of his."

Juno was married to Jupiter, king of the gods. She was a jealous wife, and Jupiter gave her good reason to be jealous. He had many affairs with goddesses and women, including one with the mortal woman Io. Juno found out, and to hide Io from Juno, Jupiter changed Io into a cow. The trick didn't work, and Juno made the hundred-eyed Argos guard Io to keep Jupiter away from her. Jupiter wanted to set Io free, so he sent the god Mercury to kill Argos. Usually, some of Argos' hundred eyes were open to watch Io, but Mercury played music that caused all one hundred eyes to close in sleep, and then Mercury killed Argos and set Io free.

The messenger exited.

Alone, Ragan said to herself, "Go about your task then, and when you have dispatched it — completed your task and dispatched my father to the Land of the Dead — I'll find a means to send you after him. You will join him in the Land of the Dead."

— 4.6 —

— Scene 18 —

The King of Cornwall and Gonorill talked together.

"I marvel that the messenger whom we sent with a letter to Cambria tarries so long there," the King of Cornwall said. "If his answer to the question why he tarried does not please us well, and if he does not show good reason for his delay, I'll teach him how to dally with his king and to detain us in such long suspense."

"My lord," Gonorill said, "I think the reason may be this: My father means to come along with him and, therefore it is my father's pleasure that the messenger shall stay so the messenger can be his attendant on the way."

"It may be so," the King of Cornwall replied, "and therefore until I know the truth of it, I will suspend my judgment."

A servant entered and said, "If it pleases your grace, an ambassador has arrived from Gallia and craves admittance to your majesty."

"From Gallia?" the King of Cornwall said. "What would his message to us concern?"

He looked at Gonorill and said, "Perhaps your father has gone to Gallia."

He then said to the servant, "Well, whatever the ambassador's message is, tell him to come in; he shall have audience with us."

The ambassador entered the room.

"What is the news from Gallia?" the King of Cornwall said. "Speak, ambassador."

"The noble King and Queen of Gallia first salute, through me, their honorable father and father-in-law, my lord Leir," the ambassador said. "Next, they commend themselves kindly to your graces, as you are people whose welfare they entirely wish. I have a letter to deliver to my lord Leir, and presents, too, if I might speak with him."

"If you might speak with him?" Gonorill said. "Why, do you think we are afraid that you should speak with him?"

"Pardon me, madam, for I don't think that," the ambassador said. "I said it only because he is not here."

"Indeed, my friend, upon some urgent cause Leir is at this time absent from the court," the King of Cornwall said, "but if you repose here a day or two, it is very likely you shall see him here, or else have certain information about where he is."

"Aren't we worthy enough to receive your message?" Gonorill asked.

"I have orders to deliver my message only to Leir," the ambassador said.

Gonorill thought, *It may be then that it will not be done quickly.*

She then said to the ambassador, "How does my sister Cordella enjoy the climate of France?"

"Exceedingly well," the ambassador said. "She has never been sick even one hour since first she set her foot upon the shore."

"I am very sorry to hear that," Gonorill said honestly.

"I hope that is not so, madam," the ambassador said.

"Didn't you say that she has always been sick since the first hour that she arrived there?" Gonorill asked.

"No, madam, I said quite the contrary," the ambassador said.

"Then I misunderstood you," Gonorill lied.

"Then Cordella is merry," the King of Cornwall said, "since she has her health."

"Oh, no," the ambassador said. "Her grief is great until the time that she can be reconciled with her father."

"May God continue it," Gonorill said honestly.

"Continue what, madam?" the ambassador asked.

"Why, her health," Gonorill lied.

"Amen to that," the ambassador said, "but may God release her grief and put her father in a better mind than to continue to be always so unkind."

"I'll be a mediator in her cause," the King of Cornwall said, "and seek all means to end his wrath."

"Madam," the ambassador said, "I hope your grace will do the like."

"Would I be a means to aggravate his wrath against my sister Cordella, whom I love so dearly?" Gonorill asked.

She then lied, "No, no."

The ambassador said, "I hope your grace will end or mitigate Leir's wrath, for he has misconceived an anger against Cordella without a cause or reason."

"Oh, yes, what else would I do?" Gonorill said.

"It's a pity it should be so," the ambassador said. "I wish it were otherwise."

"It would be a great pity it should be otherwise," Gonorill said honestly.

She wanted Leir's hatred of Cordella to continue.

"Than how, madam?" the ambassador said.

"Than that they should be reconciled again," Gonorill lied.

"Your words show that you bear an honorable mind," the ambassador said.

Gonorill thought, *My words show that your understanding is blind, and that you need an interpreter. Well, I will know your message before much longer, and I will find a way to thwart it, if I can.*

"Come in, my friend," she said, "and enjoy yourself in our court until certain information about my father comes."

— 4.7 —

— Scene 19 —

Leir and Perillus talked together. They were in the open country of Cambria, and both were carrying religious books.

"My lord, you are up today before your accustomed hour," Perillus said. "It is unusual for you to be abroad so early."

"It is unusual, indeed," Leir said. "I am so extremely tired that I can scarcely keep my eyelids open."

"And so am I, but I impute the cause to rising sooner than we are accustomed to rise," Perillus said.

"Hither my daughter means to come disguised," Leir said. "I'll sit down and read until she comes."

He sat down and began to read a religious book.

"She'll not be long, I promise you, my lord," Perillus said, "but say a couple of these robbers whom they call good-fellows step out of a hedge and set upon us. We would be 'well able' to answer them."

He was being sarcastic. Leir and he were old men and would have a hard time resisting robbers.

"It is not for us to rely upon our hands," Leir said, acknowledging that they would not be able to resist robbers.

"I am afraid that we scarcely could stand upon our legs," Perillus said. "But what could we do to defend ourselves?"

"Simply pray to God to bless us and protect us from their hands," Leir said, "for fervent prayer withstands many ill occurrences."

"I'll sit and pray with you for company," Perillus said. "Yet I have never been so sleepy in my life."

Both Leir and Perillus fell asleep.

The messenger — a potential murderer — arrived upon the scene, carrying two daggers in his hands.

He said to himself, "Wouldn't it be a mad jest if two or three of my profession should meet me and lay me down in a ditch and play rob-thief with me and by force take my gold away from me while I try to carry out this stratagem, and by this means the two gray-beards should escape? By my faith, I swear that when I would be at liberty again I would immediately go to the closest tree and hang myself."

The messenger startled when he saw Leir and Perillus.

He said to himself, "But wait, I think my 'youths' are here already and with pure religious zeal they have prayed themselves asleep. I think they know to what intent they came and they have prepared themselves for another world. It's as if they knew that they are going to be murdered and so have made themselves ready for Heaven."

The messenger took their religious books away.

He said, "Now I could stab them bravely, while they sleep, and in a manner that would put them to no pain, and by doing so, I would have showed them mighty friendship, for fear of death is worse than death itself. But my sweet queen ordered me to show this letter to them before I did the deed.

"By the Mass, they begin to stir. I'll stand aside where they can't see me. That way, I shall come upon them before they are aware of me."

Leir and Perillus woke and rose.

"I marvel that my daughter is so late in coming," Leir said.

"I am afraid that we have come to the wrong place, my lord," Perillus said.

"May God grant we don't come to harm in this place," Leir said. "I had a short nap, but my dream was so full of dread that I am much amazed to think about it."

"Fear not, my lord," Perillus said. "Dreams are only fantasies and slight imaginations of the brain."

Unseen by them, the messenger said to himself about Perillus, "Persuade Leir so, but I'll make him and you confess that dreams often prove to be too true."

"Please, my lord," Perillus said, "what was the content of your dream? I may go near to guess what it portends."

"Leave that to me," the messenger said to himself. "I will explain the dream."

"I thought that my daughters, Gonorill and Ragan, stood both before me with such grim faces," Leir said, "each brandishing a sword in their hands, ready to lop off a limb where the sword fell, and in their other hands each held a naked dagger, with which they stabbed me in a hundred places, and to their thinking, left me there for dead. But then my youngest daughter, fair Cordella, came with a box of medicinal ointment in her hand, and poured it into my bleeding wounds, and by those good means I was recovered and well, in perfect health, as formerly I was. And with the fear of this I awoke, and still for fear my feeble joints quake."

The messenger said out loud, "I'll make you quake for something right now. Stand, stand!"

Leir and Perillus whirled around.

"We do, my friend," Leir said, "although with much difficulty."

"Deliver, deliver!" the messenger said.

This meant to deliver, or hand over, your valuables.

"Deliver us, good Lord, from such as he," Perillus said.

"You should have prayed before, while it was the time for prayer," the messenger said, "and then perhaps you might have escaped my hands. But you, like 'faithful' watchmen, fell asleep while I came and took your halberds from you. And now you lack your weapons of defense."

He showed them the religious books he had taken from them. A halberd is a weapon, but the messenger meant the religious books that Leir and Perillus had been reading. Apparently the messenger believed that holding a religious book provided defense against evil.

The messenger continued, "How have you any hope to be delivered? This comes because you had no better staying power; you fell asleep when you should watch and pray."

Matthew 26:41 states, "*Watch, and pray, that ye enter not into temptation: the spirit indeed is ready, but the flesh is weak*" (1599 Geneva Bible).

"My friend," Leir said, "you seem to be a proper man."

"By God's blood," the messenger said, "how the old slave claws me by the elbow! He thinks, perhaps, to escape from me by acting obsequiously toward me."

"And, it may be," Perillus said, "that you are in some need of money."

"I can show that to be false," the messenger said. "Behold my evidence."

He showed them the moneybags that he had gotten from Ragan.

"If I have anything that will do you any good," Leir said, "I will give it to you, even with a very good will."

The messenger took the moneybag that Leir offered him.

"Here, take mine, too," Perillus said, "and I wish with all my heart, to make you happy, that the amount of money I have were twice as much."

The messenger took Perillus' moneybag, and then he weighed Leir's moneybag and Perillus' moneybag in his hands.

"I don't want them," the messenger said. "They are too light for me."

He put both moneybags in his pockets.

"Why, then, farewell," Leir said, "and if you have any occasion to employ me to have discussions with the queen, it is likely enough that I can make you happy."

Leir and Perillus attempted to leave.

The messenger stopped them and asked, "Do you hear? Do you hear, sir? If I have any occasion to employ you to have discussions with the queen, would you do one thing for me, if I should ask?"

"Yes, anything that lies within my power," Leir said. "Here is my hand upon it."

Leir shook hands with the messenger, and then he said, "And so farewell."

Leir and Perillus attempted to leave.

The messenger stopped them and said, "Listen, sir. Please, let me have a word with you. I think that a comely honest ancient man such as you ought not to lie to someone such as me in order to get an advantage. I know that when you shall come to do what you promised that you will recant all that you have said and promised to me."

"Don't mistrust him, but test his promise whenever you will," Perillus said. "Leir is Ragan's father, and therefore he may do much good for you."

"I know he is Ragan's father," the messenger said, "and therefore I intend to test his words. You are his friend, too; I must test you both."

"Please do," Leir and Perillus said. "Please do."

Leir and Perillus attempted to leave.

The messenger stopped them and said, "Stop, gray-beards, then, and prove to me that you are men of your words. Queen Ragan has tied me by a solemn oath here in this place to see you both dispatched.

"Now, for the safeguard of my conscience, do me the pleasure of killing yourselves; that way, you shall save me the labor of having to do it, and you shall prove that you yourselves are old men who are true to your words.

"And here I vow, in sight of all the world, that if you kill yourselves, I will never trouble you again as long as I live."

"Frighten us not with terror, my good friend," Leir said, "nor strike such fear into our aged hearts. Don't play the role of the cat that plays with the mouse and then suddenly makes her a prey, but if you are marked for the man of death to me and to my Damon, tell me plainly, so that we may be prepared for the stroke and make ourselves fit for the world-to-come by praying."

Leir was alluding to the story of the very close friends Damon and Pythias.

Pythias was accused of plotting against Dionysius I, the tyrant of Syracuse, and was sentenced to death. Damon knew that Pythias needed to go home and put his affairs in order and say goodbye to family and friends before dying, so he volunteered to be a hostage to guarantee Pythias' return. If Pythias should fail to return by a certain date, Damon would die in his place. Dionysius I agreed, and Pythias left and then returned by the agreed-upon date. Impressed by the two friends' loyalty to each other, Dionysius I decided to allow both of them to live.

"I am the last of any mortal race that your eyes are ever likely to behold," the messenger said, "and I was sent here on purpose to this place to give a final period to your days, which are so wicked; you have lived a wicked life so long that your own children seek to shorten your life."

"Did you come from France with the purpose of killing me?" Leir asked.

He believed that Cordella must have sent an assassin to kill him.

"From France?" the messenger said, insulted. "By God's wounds, do I look like a Frenchman? Surely I am not wearing my own face: Somebody has exchanged faces with me without my knowing it. But I am sure that my apparel is entirely English. Sirrah, what do you mean by asking me that question? I could spoil the appearance of this face because of my anger. A French face!"

"I ask you because my daughter Cordella, whom I have offended, and at whose hands I have deserved as ill as ever any father did from a child, is the Queen of France, no thanks at all to me," Leir said. "The thanks for her being the Queen of France goes all to God, Who sees my injustice. If it is the case that she seeks revenge against me, as with good reason she may justly do, I will most willingly resign my life. I will be a sacrifice to mitigate her anger.

"I will never entreat you to forgive me because I am unworthy to live. Therefore, speak soon, and I will soon make speed, perhaps to die. Tell me whether Cordella ordered you to do this deed."

"As I am a perfect gentleman, I say that you are speaking French to me," the messenger said. "I have never heard Cordella's name before, nor have I ever been in France in all my life. I never knew you had a daughter there to whom you have proven to be so unkind a churl. But your own tongue declares that you have been a vile old wretch, and full of heinous sin."

"Ah, no, my friend," Leir said, "much you are deceived. Except for Cordella, whom I confess I wronged through doting frenzy and too jealous love, no one lives under Heaven's bright eye — the sun — who can convict me of impiety.

"And, therefore, surely you are mistaken, for I am in true peace with all the world."

"You are the fitter for the King of Heaven," the messenger said, "and, therefore, to rid you of suspense, know that the Queen of Cambria and the Queen of Cornwall, your own two daughters, Gonorill and Ragan, have ordered me to massacre you here.

"Why would you then try to persuade me just now that you are in Christian love with all the world, when your own children hate you so much that they have hired me to abridge your fate by shortening your life?

"Oh, damn such vile, dissembling, lying breath that wants to deceive even at the point of death."

"Am I awake, or is this only a dream?" Perillus asked.

"Fear nothing, man," the messenger said. "You are only in a dream, and you shall never wake up until Doomsday — the Day of Judgment. By then, I hope, you will have slept enough."

"Yet, gentle friend," Leir said, "grant one thing before I die."

"I'll grant you anything except your lives," the messenger said.

"Oh, just assure me by some certain token that my two daughters hired you to do this deed," Leir said. "If I were once convinced that they have, then I would wish for life no longer, but instead I would crave to die."

"That it is true that your two daughters have hired me to murder you, in the sight of Heaven I swear," the messenger said.

"Swear not by Heaven for fear of punishment," Leir said. "The Heavens are guiltless of such heinous acts."

"I swear by the Earth, the mother of us all," the messenger said.

"Swear not by the Earth," Leir said, "for she abhors to bear such bastards as are murderers of her sons."

"Why, then," the messenger said, "by Hell and all the devils, I swear."

"Swear not by Hell," Leir said, "for that stands gaping wide to swallow you if you do this deed."

Matthew 5:33-37 (1599 Geneva Bible) discusses swearing:

33 Again, ye have heard that it was said to them of old time, Thou shalt not forswear thyself, but shalt perform thine oaths to the Lord.

34 But I say unto you, Swear not at all, neither by heaven, for it is the throne of God:

35 Nor yet by the earth, for it is his footstool: neither by Jerusalem: for it is the city of the great King.

36 Neither shalt thou swear by thine head, because thou canst not make one hair white or black.

37 But let your communication be Yea, yea: Nay, nay. For whatsoever is more than these, cometh of evil.

Thunder sounded and lightning flashed.

The messenger thought, *I wish that word "Hell" were in his belly again. It has frightened me even to the very heart. This old man is some strong magician: His words have turned my mind away from this exploit. I no longer want to commit these murders.*

He said out loud, "Then neither the Heavens, nor Earth, nor Hell be witness, but let this paper witness for them all."

He gave Leir Gonorill's letter.

As Leir and Perillus read the letter, the messenger thought, *Shall I relent, or shall I prosecute? Shall I resolve, or would it be better for me to recant? I will not crack my credit with two queens to whom I have already given my word. Oh, but my conscience tells me that if I commit these murders, I will get Heaven's hate, Earth's scorn, and Hell's pains.*

Leir and Perillus blessed themselves — they made the sign of the cross.

"Oh, just Jehovah," Perillus said, "Whose almighty power governs all things in this spacious world, how can you suffer such outrageous acts to be committed without just revenge? Oh, viperous and accursed generation — to seek his blood whose blood did make them first!"

Gonorill and Ragan were seeking the blood of their father, who had helped bring them into existence.

"Ah, my true friend in all extremity," Leir said to Perillus, "let us submit ourselves to the will of God. Things past all sense, let us not seek to know: It is God's will, and therefore it must be so."

He then said to the messenger, "My friend, I am prepared for the stroke of your dagger. Strike when you will, and I forgive you here, even from the very bottom of my heart."

"But I am not prepared to strike you dead," the messenger said.

"Farewell, Perillus," Leir said. "You were even the truest friend who ever lived in adversity. The last kindness I'll request of you is that you go to my daughter Cordella and carry her father's last blessing to her. Also request from her that she will forgive me, for I have wronged her without any cause."

He then prayed, "Now, Lord, receive me, for I come to you, and I die, I hope, in perfect Christian love."

He then said to the messenger, "Kill me now, I ask you. Kill me. I have lived too long."

"Yes," the messenger said, "but you are unwise to send an errand by a man who will never be able to deliver it. Why, he must go along with you to Heaven. It would not be good if you should go all alone."

"No doubt Perillus shall go to Heaven, when, by the course of nature, he must surrender his due to death. But that time shall not come until God permits it to come."

"No, that time shall come immediately," the messenger said. "I have a 'passport' for him in my pocket, already sealed, and he must necessarily ride posthaste to Heaven with you."

The messenger showed Leir the "passport": a moneybag.

"The letter that I read did not say so," Leir said. "It stated only that I must die; there was no word about Perillus."

"True," the messenger said, "but the queen commands it must be so, and I have been paid for him as well as for you."

"I, who have borne you company in life," Perillus said to Leir, "most willingly will bear a share in death. It doesn't matter about me."

He then said to the messenger, "It doesn't matter about me even a whit, nor would it matter for a hundred such as you and me."

"By the Virgin Mary, I say it does matter, sir, with your permission," the messenger replied. "Your good days are past. Though death does not matter for you, it does matter for me. Proper, handsome men are not so disposed to die."

"Oh, but beware how you lay your hand upon the high anointed of the Lord," Perillus said. "Oh, think about your actions before you begin. Dispatch me immediately, but don't meddle with him."

People in this society believed in the divine right of kings: Kings become kings by the will of God.

1 Samuel 26:9 states, "*And David said to Abishai, Destroy him not: for who can lay his hand on the Lord's anointed, and be guiltless?*" (1599 Geneva Bible).

2 Samuel 1:14-16 (1599 Geneva Bible) states this:

14 And David said unto him, How wast thou not afraid, to put forth thine hand to destroy the Anointed of the Lord?

15 Then David called one of his young men, and said, Go near, and fall upon him. And he smote him that he died.

16 Then said David unto him, Thy blood be upon thine own head: for thine own mouth hath testified against thee, saying, I have slain the Lord's Anointed.

"Friend, your orders are to deal with me, and I am that man who has deserved all that is coming to him," Leir said to the messenger. "The plot was laid to take away my life, and here my life is: I ask you to take it. Yet, for my sake, and as you are a man, spare this my friend who hither with me came. I brought him forth to a place where he would not have been except for his good will to bear me company. He left his friends, his country, and his goods, and he came with me in very hard times.

"Oh, if he should miscarry here and die, who is the cause of it, except only I?"

"Why, I am the cause of his death," the messenger said. "Let that never trouble you."

"Oh, no," Leir said, "it is I who would have caused his death. Oh, if I now were able to give you the monarchy of all the spacious world in order to save his life, I would bestow it on you and make you king of everything, but I have nothing except these tears and prayers, and the submission of a bended knee."

Leir knelt before the messenger and begged, "Oh, if all this moves your mind to show mercy, spare him! In Heaven you shall find similar mercy."

The messenger thought, *I am as hard to be moved as another, and yet I think the strength of their persuasions moves me a little to show mercy.*

"My friend," Perillus said, "if fear of the almighty power has the power to move you, we have said enough, but if your mind can be persuaded with gold to show mercy, we don't have it at present to give to you.

"Yet to yourself you may do a greater good if you keep your hands still undefiled from blood, for consider well with yourself, when you have finished this outrageous act, what horror always will haunt you for the deed.

"Think also about this, that they who would incense you to be the butcher of their father, when it is done, for fear it should be known would find a way to rid you from the world — they will have you murdered.

"Oh, then you will be forever tied in chains of everlasting torments to endure, even in the hottest hole of grisly Hell, such pains as never mortal tongue can tell."

Thunder sounded.

The messenger trembled from fear, and he let fall the dagger that was in his hand closest to Perillus.

"Oh, the Heavens be thanked, he will spare my friend!" Leir said. "Now, when you will, come make an end of me."

The messenger let fall the other dagger.

"Oh, happy sight!" Perillus said. "He means to save my lord! May the King of Heaven help him continue in this good mind!"

"Why do you hesitate to do the execution?" Leir asked. "Why don't you kill me?"

"I am as willful as you concerning your life," the messenger replied. "I will not do it, even though now you entreat me to kill you."

"Ah, now I see you have some spark of grace," Perillus said.

"Curse you two for it; you two have put it in me!" the messenger said. "You two are the most dangerously clever old men that ever I heard! Well, to speak plainly, I'll not meddle with you. Here I found you, and here I'll leave you. If anyone should ask you why you are still alive, say that your tongues were better than your hands."

The messenger exited.

"Farewell," Perillus said as the messenger left. "If we ever meet again, it shall take a lot of effort, but I will you re-greet."

Although the messenger had intended to kill the two men, in the end he had shown them mercy. For that reason, Perillus was willing to greet the messenger if they ever met again, although it would take an effort of the will.

He then said to Leir, "Courage, my lord, the worst is over and past. Let us give thanks to God, and hurry away from here."

"You are deceived," Leir said, "for I am past the best and I don't know whither we can go to from here. Death would have been better welcome to me than a longer life in which to add more misery."

"It would not be good to return from whence we came," Perillus said. "We ought not to go back again to your daughter Ragan. Now let us go to France, to Cordella, your youngest daughter; doubtless she will help you."

"Oh, how can I persuade myself of that," Leir said, "since my other two daughters are quite devoid of love? To those two daughters I was so kind. My gifts ought to make them love me, if nothing else."

"No worldly gifts, but grace from God on high, nourishes virtue and true charity," Perillus said. "Remember well what words Cordella spoke that time you asked her how she loved your grace. She said her love to you was as much as a child ought to bear her father."

"But she did find that my love was not to her as a father should bear a child," Leir said.

"That doesn't make her love be any less, if she loves you as a child should," Perillus said. "You have tried two daughters; try one more for my sake. I'll never entreat you to further trial make. Remember well the dream you had of late, and think about what comfort it foretells to us."

"Come, truest friend whom ever man possessed," Leir said. "I know you advise all things for the best. If this third daughter plays a kinder part, it comes from God, and not from my merit and desert."

— 4.8 —

— Scene 20 —

Alone, the Gallian ambassador said this to himself:

"Recently, news has come to the court that old Lord Leir remains in Cambria. I'll hurry there immediately to give my letter and my message to him.

"I never have been less welcome in a place in all my lifetime than I have been here. The stately Queen Gonorill especially made me unwelcome; she would not cast one gracious look on me, but always, with scowling and suspicious eyes, she would take exceptions at each word I spoke, and gladly she would have undermined and compromised me to know the information that I as ambassador bring to old Lord Leir.

"But she is likely to angrily hop without her hope being satisfied, and in this matter she will lack what she wants, although according to reports I have heard, she'll have what she wants in all other matters.

"Well, I will ride away for Cambria; within these few days I hope to be there."

CHAPTER 5

— 5.1 —

— Scene 21 —

The King of Gallia, Cordella, and Mumford talked together in a room in the King of Gallia's castle.

The King of Gallia said, "By this time, our father-in-law understands our mind and our kind greetings sent to him recently. Therefore, my mind foretells that before long, we shall receive from Britain happy news."

He thought that by this time, his ambassador had delivered the letter to Leir, and he was hoping that Leir would come to Gallia.

"I fear my sister will dissuade his mind," Cordella said, "for she to me has always been unkind."

"Fear not, my love," the King of Gallia said. "Since if we should know the worst, the most recent means helps if we miss the first."

He meant that if their letter did not persuade Leir to come to Gallia, then they would try again to persuade him to come. If the first attempt didn't work, then perhaps the next one would.

The King of Gallia added, "If Leir will not come to Gallia to us, then we will sail to Britain to him."

"Well, if I once see Britain again," Mumford said, "I have sworn I'll never come home without my wench, and I'll not be forsworn and perjured; I'd rather never come home while I live."

"Are you sure, Mumford," Cordella asked, "that she is still a maiden?"

The word "maiden" meant both 1) unmarried woman, and 2) virgin. In this society, the two meanings were supposed to go together.

"No, I'll not swear she is a maiden, but she passes for one," Mumford said. "I'll take and marry her despite the risk that she is not a maiden, if I can get her."

"Yes, that's well put in," Cordella said.

71

By "well put in," Cordella meant "well said," or "well put in this conversation," but Mumford took the phrase in a bawdy sense.

"Well put in?" Mumford said. "No, it was ill put in, for had it been as well put in as ever I put it in, in all my days, I would have made her follow me to France."

"No, you'd have been so kind as to take her with you," Cordella said, "or else, were I she, I would have been so 'loving' as I'd stay behind in England without you. Yet I must confess that you are a very proper, handsome man and you are able to make a wench do more than she would do."

The words "do more than she would do" are ambiguous and can mean 1) do more than she would normally do, or 2) do more than she wants to do.

"Well, I have a pair of baggy trousers that will serve the purpose of holding all of your mocks at me," Mumford said.

"We see you have handsome trousers," the King of Gallia said.

"Yes, and of the newest fashion," Cordella added.

"More insults, more!" Mumford said. "Continue to put them in my trousers! They'll serve instead of padding, but don't put in too many, lest the trousers' seams crack and your insults fly out among you again. You must not think to outface me so easily in my attempt to win my loved one, whom if I see once again, ten teams of horses shall not draw me away from her until I have full and whole possession."

Mumford being Mumford, he probably also meant hole possession.

"True, but only one team and a cart will be enough to serve the purpose," the King of Gallia said.

"Not only for him, but also for his wench," Cordella said.

She was referring to the practice of punishing prostitutes by forcing them to walk behind a cart they were tied to. Sometimes, they were whipped as they walked, and sometimes they were taken to a place where they would be whipped.

"Well, you are two to one," Mumford said. "I give up; and since I see you so pleasantly disposed, which indeed is but seldom seen, I'll claim a promise of you that you shall not deny me, for promise is debt, and by this hand" — he raised his hand in the air as if he were swearing an oath in court — "you promised it to me, and therefore you owe it to me, and you shall pay it to me, or I'll sue you upon an action of unkindness."

"Please, Lord Mumford, tell me what promise I made to you?" the King of Gallia asked.

"Indeed, nothing but this," Mumford said. "You promised that during the next fair weather, which is right now, you would go in progress down to the seaside, which is very near."

To "progress" means to travel, but for a high-ranking official such as a king, it often meant to make a state journey, which was very ceremonious. Mumford wanted to go to the seashore and then sail to England.

"Indeed, in this proposal I will join with you," the King of Gallia said, "and be a mediator to my queen."

He said to his wife, Cordella, "Please, my love, let this proposal go forward. My mind foretells that it will be a lucky voyage."

"Entreaty is not necessary where you may command," Cordella said. "As long as you are pleased, I am very well content. Yet as much as I desire to see the sea, by that much am I most unwilling to be seen."

"We'll go disguised, all unknown to everyone," the King of Gallia said.

"Howsoever you make one in this traveling group, I'll make another," Cordella said.

"And I will make the third," Mumford said. "Oh, I am overjoyed! See what power love has, which gets with a word what all the world besides could never obtain! But what disguises shall we have, my lord?"

"Indeed," the King of Gallia said, "my queen and I will be disguised like a plain country couple, and you shall be Roger, our serving-man, and wait upon us."

Mumford made a face.

The King of Gallia added, "Or, if you prefer, you shall be the master, and we will wait on you."

"It's about time!" Mumford said. "This plan is excellent. Come, let's get started."

— 5.2 —

— Scene 22 —

The King of Cambria and Ragan talked together. Some nobles were present.

The King of Cambria asked, "What strange mischance or unexpected happening has thus deprived us of our father-in-law's presence? Can no man tell us what's become of Leir, with whom we talked not two days ago?

"My lords, let everywhere horse-mounted soldiers be sent to scour through all our kingdom. Dispatch a post-messenger immediately to the King of Cornwall to see if any news can be found about Leir there.

"I myself will make a strict inquiry here, and all about our cities near at hand, until certain news of where he is staying is brought to me."

The nobles exited to carry out their orders.

"All sorrow is but a counterfeit compared to my sorrow," Ragan said. "My lips are almost sealed up with grief. My sorrow is the real substance while their sorrow only seems to weep the loss that tears cannot redeem.

"Oh, never was heard so strange a misadventure, a thing so far beyond the reach of reason, since no man's reason can speculate about the cause that has removed my father thus away from here.

"Oh, I fear that some charm or invocation of wicked spirits or infernal fiends, stirred up by Cordella, moves this change and brings my father prematurely to his end.

"But if I might know that the detested witch were certainly the cause of this uncertain ill, I myself to France would go in some disguise and with these fingernails scratch out her hateful eyes, for since I am deprived of my father, I loathe my life and wish my death the rather."

"The Heavens are just and hate impiety," the King of Cambria said. "And they will no doubt reveal such heinous, wicked crimes. Do not censure and judge anyone until you know the right: Let Him be judge Who brings truth to light."

"Oh, but my grief, like a swelling tide," Ragan said, "exceeds the bounds of common patience, nor can I moderate my tongue so much to conceal them whom I suspect."

"This matter shall be closely examined," the King of Cambria said. "If Cordella is at fault, a thousand Frances shall not harbor her."

The Gallian ambassador entered the room and said, "All happiness to the Cambrian King."

"Welcome, my friend," the King of Cambria said. "From whence have you come as ambassador?"

"From Gallia I was sent to Cornwall with a letter to Leir, your honorable father-in-law. Because I did not find him there as I had expected, I was directed hither to go."

"Frenchman," Ragan asked, "what is your message to my father?"

"My letter, madam, will state the message," the Gallian ambassador said. "My orders are to deliver the letter."

"In his absence you may trust us with your letter," Ragan said.

"I must perform my charge in such a manner as I have strict orders from my king," the Gallian ambassador said.

"Your king and you have been plotting," Ragan said. "You need not come here to ask for Leir. You know where he is better than we ourselves do."

"Madam, I hope he is not far away," the Gallian ambassador said.

"Has the young murderess, your outrageous queen," Ragan said, "no means to disguise her detested deeds in finishing my guiltless father's days — because he gave her nothing to be her dowry — but by the color of a feigned reason for an embassy to send a letter to him here at our court?

"Go carry the letter to them who sent it here, and tell them to keep their scrolls to themselves. They cannot blind us with such a slight excuse to smother up such monstrous vile abuse.

"And, were it not that it is against the law of arms to offer violence to a messenger who has diplomatic immunity, we would inflict such torments on you as would force you to reveal the truth."

"Madam, your threats not even a little appall my mind," the Gallian ambassador said. "I know that my conscience is guiltless of this act that you accuse me of. My king and queen, I dare be sworn, are free from any thought of such impiety.

"And, therefore, madam, you have done them wrong, and that is ill-befitting your sister's love. Cordella, simply out of the duty that a child owes her father, tenderly loves Leir as much as ever you respected him for giving you your dowry. The king your husband will not say as much as you have said against the King and Queen of France."

"I will suspend my judgment until such a time that more evidence gives us further light into this matter," the King of Cambria said. "Yet, to speak plainly, your coming here inspired a great suspicion in our doubting mind that you resemble, to be brief, a man who first robs and then cries, 'Stop the thief.'"

"I pray to God that someone near you has not done what you just said," the Gallian ambassador said.

Ragan said, "Leave, rude fellow, and reply no more to us" — she hit the Gallian ambassador — "for the law of arms shall not protect your tongue."

"Never have I been treated with such discourtesy!" the Gallian ambassador said. "God and my king, I trust, before very long, will find a way to remedy this wrong."

He exited.

"How shall I live to endure such disgrace at every base and vulgar peasant's hands?" Ragan said. "It ill suits my imperial state to be thus treated, and have no man take my part."

She wept.

"What should I do?" the King of Cambria said. "If I were to violate the law of arms, it would cause me everlasting disgrace, but I will take revenge upon his master, the King of Gallia, who sent him here to try to delude us."

"If you put up with this," Ragan said, "you can be sure that before long, now that my father has thus been murdered, Cordella will come and claim a third part of your crown as due to her by inheritance."

Ragan's words stated that she believed that Leir was dead and that Cordella was a parricide: Cordella had caused the death of Leir, her father. Of course, Ragan was lying about Cordella.

"But I will prove that her title is nothing but the shame and the reward of parricide," the King of Cambria said, "and I will make her an example to the world for the ages-to-come to be astonished at her punishment. This will I do, as I am Cambria's king, or I will lose my life as I attempt to get revenge for Leir.

"Come, first let's learn what the news is about our father and father-in-law, and then we will proceed as best fits the situation."

— 5.3 —

— Scene 23 —

Leir, Perillus, and two sailors who were wearing sea clothing, including sea caps, talked. They were in Gallia.

"My honest friends," Perillus said, "we are ashamed to show the great extreme conditions of our present state, in that at this time we are brought so low that we lack money to pay our passage. The truth is this: We met with some robbers, a little before we came aboard your ship. These robbers stripped us entirely of all the money we had and left us not even a penny in our moneybags. Yet, despite lacking money, we will find a way to see you satisfied to the uttermost."

The first mariner looked at Leir and especially at the clothing he was wearing.

He said, "Here's a good jacket. It would look very good on me. I would be fine-looking in it."

The second mariner looked at Perillus and especially at the clothing he was wearing.

He said, "Here's a good cloak. I wonder how I would look in it."

"Indeed," Leir said, "had we other clothing to supply their place, even if they were mean clothes, we would willingly give you these articles of clothing."

"Listen, sir," the first mariner said to Leir. "You look like an honest man. I'll not refrain from doing you a pleasure. Here's a good, strong, multi-colored gabardine jacket, which cost me fourteen good shillings at Billingsgate. Give me your jacket for it, and your cap for mine, and I'll forgive the fee for your passage."

"With all my heart and twenty thanks," Leir said.

Leir and the first mariner exchanged jackets and caps.

The second mariner said to Perillus, "Listen, sir. You shall have a better bargain than your friend because you are my friend. Here is a good russet-colored wool sea-jacket. It will bide more stress, I warrant you, than two of his. Yet, because you seem to be an honest gentleman, I am content to exchange it for your cloak, and I ask you nothing more for your passage."

He pulled off Perillus' cloak.

"My own clothing I willingly would exchange with you," Perillus replied, "and think myself indebted to your kindness, but I wish that my friend might still keep his garment."

He then said to the first mariner, "My friend the mariner, I'll give you this new jacket if you will restore my friend's jacket back to him again."

"No," the first mariner said. "If I do that, then I wish that I might never again eat powdered beef — beef preserved in salt — and mustard, nor drink a can of good liquor while I live. My friend, you have little reason to seek to hinder me from getting my bargain, but the best thing is, a bargain's a bargain."

Leir said quietly to Perillus, "Kind friend, it is much better as it is, for by this means we may escape unknown until we find the right time and opportunity."

The second mariner said to the first mariner, "Look! Look! They are laying their heads together; they'll repent their bargain soon. It would be best for us to go while we are able."

The first mariner said to Leir, "May God be with you, sir. As for your passage back again, I'll treat you as unreasonably as I would another person."

"I know you will," Leir replied, "but we hope to bring ready money with us when we come back again."

The mariners exited.

Leir said to Perillus, "Were men ever in this extreme condition, in a strange country, and devoid of friends, and with not even a penny to help ourselves? Kind friend, what do you think will become of us?"

"Be of good cheer, my lord," Perillus said. "I have a jacket that will yield us money enough to get us what we need until we come to your daughter Cordella's court, and then, I hope, we shall find friends enough."

"Ah, kind Perillus," Leir said, "there is something I fear, and it makes me faint before I come there.

"Can kindness spring out of ingratitude, or love be reaped where hatred has been sown?

"Can poisonous henbane join in league with sweet-tasting mithridate, or sugar grow in wormwood's bitter stalk?"

Mithridate is made of many ingredients that promote good health.

Leir continued, "It cannot be: they are too opposite, and so am I to any kindness here. I have thrown wormwood on the sugared youth, and similar to henbane, poisoned the fountain whence flowed the sweet mithridate of a child's good will.

"I, like an envious thorn, have pricked the heart and turned sweet grapes to sour, unrelished fruits.

"The without-a-cause anger of my discourteous breast has soured the sweet milk of Dame Nature's breasts.

"My bitter words have galled her honey thoughts, and weeds of rancor have choked the flower of grace.

"So then what remainder is there of any hope? Instead, all our fortunes will go quite aslope."

"Fear not, my lord," Perillus said. "The perfect good indeed can never be corrupted by the bad. A new fresh vessel still retains the taste of that which first is poured into the same. And therefore, although you name yourself the thorn, the weed, the gall, the henbane, and the wormwood, yet Cordella will continue in her former state, which is that of the honey, milk, grape, sugar, and mithridate."

"You pleasing orator to me in my woe, cease to beguile me with your hopeful speeches," Leir said. "Oh, join with me and think of nothing but crosses, and then we'll each lament the other's losses."

"Why say the worst?" Perillus said. "The worst can be but death, and to suffer death is better than to suffer despair. So then risk death, which may convert to life."

After death, one may enjoy ever-lasting life. Or one may not die, and things will get better.

Perillus continued, "Banish despair, which brings a thousand deaths."

"Overcome with your strong arguments, I yield to you, and I will be directed by you, as you will," Leir said. "As you yield comfort to my crazed thoughts, I wish I could yield comfort to your body, which is very weak, I know, and ill-requited because of lack of fresh meat and due sustenance."

"It's a pity, my lord," Perillus said. "My heart bleeds to think that you should be in such extremely poor circumstances."

"Come, let us go and see what God will send," Leir said. "When all means fail, He is the surest friend."

— 5.4 —

— Scene 24 —

The King of Gallia, Cordella, and Mumford were disguised as country folk. Mumford carried a picnic basket and a portable folding table. They were near the seashore of Gallia.

The King of Gallia said to Cordella, "This tedious journey all on foot, sweet love, cannot be pleasing to your tender joints, which never were used to these toilsome walks."

"I have never in my life taken more delight in any journey than I do in this," Cordella replied. "It did me good when we happened to come among the merry crew of country folk and see what industry and pains they took to win for themselves commendations among their friends.

"Lord, how they labor to bestir themselves, and in their quirky, peculiar behavior to go beyond the moon, aka go to extravagant lengths, and so behave with such bizarre fits that one would think they were beside their wits!"

She then said to Mumford, who was performing the role of Roger, an attendant, "Come away now, Roger, with your basket."

"Be quiet, dame," Mumford said. "Here comes a couple of old 'youths.'"

He added, "I must grow fat, aka entertain myself, with jesting at them."

Leir and Perillus entered the scene, walking very feebly because of weakness from hunger.

"No," Cordella said, "please don't make fun of them. They seem to be men who are much overwhelmed with grief and misery. Let's stand aside and listen to what they say."

Cordella, the King of Gallia, and Mumford stood to the side and listened to Leir and Perillus.

"Ah, my Perillus," Leir said, "now I see we both shall end our days on this unfruitful soil."

They were not receiving sustenance — physical or spiritual — on this soil and so it was unfruitful for them.

He continued, "Oh, I faint for lack of sustenance, and you, I know, are in little better condition. No gentle tree affords one taste of fruit to comfort us until we meet with men. No lucky path conducts our luckless steps to a place where any comfort dwells. May sweet rest befall our happy souls, for here I see our bodies must have their end."

"Ah, my dear lord," Perillus said, "how my heart laments to see you brought to the furthest point of adversity! Oh, if you love me, as you do profess, or have ever thought well of me in my life" — he shoved his sleeves high on his arms — "feed on this flesh, whose veins are not so dry but there is nutriment left to comfort you. Oh, feed on this; if this will do you good, I'll smile for joy to see you suck my blood."

"I am no cannibal that I should delight to slake my hungry jaws with human flesh," Leir said. "I am no devil, or ten times worse than so, to suck the blood of such a peerless friend. Oh, do not think that I respect my life as dearly as I do your loyal love."

He added, "Ah, Britain, I shall never see you anymore, you that have unkindly banished your king, and yet it is not you that makes me complain, but instead it is they who were nearer to me than you are."

"What do I hear?" Cordella said. "This lamenting voice, I think, before now I often have heard."

She had not recognized her father because he had changed through suffering and because he was wearing mariners' clothing.

"Ah, Gonorill," Leir said, "was the gift of half my kingdom the reason that you sought to have my life?

"Ah, cruel Ragan, did I give you everything, and everything could not suffice without you also wanting my blood?

"Ah, poor Cordella, did I give you nothing, and never shall I be able to give you anything?

"Oh, let me warn all ages that ensue how people trust flattery and reject the truth.

"Well, unkind girls, I here forgive you both — yet the just Heavens will hardly do the like — and I only crave forgiveness, at the end, of good Cordella, and of you, my friend.

"I crave the forgiveness of God, whose Majesty I have offended many thousand ways by my sin.

"I crave the forgiveness of her, dear heart, Cordella, whom I for no reason turned out of all her inheritance through flatterers' persuasion.

"I crave the forgiveness of you, kind friend, Perillus, who, but for me, I know, would have never come to this place of woe."

"It's a pity that I should ever live to see my noble father in this misery," Cordella said.

"Sweet love, don't reveal who you are as yet," the King of Gallia said, "until we know the source of all this ill."

"Oh, but some food, some food!" Cordella said. "Don't you see how near they are to death for lack of food?"

Cordella took Mumford's picnic basket and put the food on the portable folding table.

Perillus prayed, "Lord, Who helped Your servants in their need, either now or never send us help speedily."

He saw the table and food, and he also saw Cordella, the King of Gallia, and Mumford, all of whom were disguised as country folk.

He then said to Leir, "Oh, comfort, comfort! Yonder is a banquet and men and women, my lord; be of good cheer, for I see comfort coming very near. Oh, my lord, a banquet and men and women!"

"Oh, let kind pity mollify their hearts," Leir said, "so that they may help us in our great need."

"May God save you, friends," Perillus said to the disguised Cordella, the King of Gallia, and Mumford, "and if this blessed banquet affords any food or sustenance, even for His sake Who saved us all from death, please graciously save us from the grip of famine."

The disguised Cordella pointed to the food and said, "Here, father, sit and eat; here, sit and drink, and I wish that it were far better for your sakes."

In this culture, a person could call an old man "father" simply as a title of respect despite not being biologically related to him.

Perillus took Leir by the hand and led him to the table.

"I'll give you thanks soon," Perillus said to Cordella. "My friend is fainting and needs immediate help."

Leir drank.

Mumford thought, *I bet that he won't wait to say grace before he eats. Oh, there's no sauce comparable to a hungry stomach to make food taste good.*

"The blessed God of Heaven has thought about us," Perillus said.

"Thanks be to Him and to these kind courteous folk," Leir said, "by whose humanity we are preserved."

They ate hungrily. Leir drank.

Cordella said about Leir's drink, "And may that draught be to him as was that draught that old Aeson drank, which renewed his withered age and made him young again."

In the myth of Jason and the Golden Fleece, Jason brought the Golden Fleece and the young witch Medea to his home. Medea made a medicinal draught that restored youth to Jason's aged father, Aeson.

Cordella continued, "And may that food be to him as was that food that the prophet Elijah ate, and with the strength it gave him he walked forty days and never fainted."

1 Kings 19:4-8 (1599 Geneva Bible) states this:

4 But he went a day's journey into the wilderness, and came and sat down under a Juniper tree, and desired that he might die, and said, It is now enough: O Lord, take my soul, for I am no better than my fathers.

5 And as he lay and slept under the Juniper tree, behold now, an Angel touched him, and said unto him, Up, and eat.

6 And when he looked about, behold, there was a cake baken on the coals, and a pot of water at his head: so he did eat and drink, and returned and slept.

7 And the Angel of the Lord came again the second time, and touched him, and said, Up, and eat: for thou hast a great journey.

8 Then he arose, and did eat and drink, and walked in the strength of that meat forty days and forty nights, unto Horeb the mount of God.

Cordella then asked her husband, the King of Gallia, "Shall I conceal my identity longer from my father? Or shall I tell him who I am?"

"Wait a while for his strength to return," the King of Gallia said, "lest being overjoyed with seeing you, his poor weak senses should forsake their office and so our cause of joy be turned to sorrow."

He was afraid that Leir's joy at seeing Cordella in his weakened state could cause him to go mad or to suffer a stroke or heart attack and die.

"How are you, my lord?" Perillus asked. "How do you feel?"

"I think I never ate such tasty food," Leir said. "It is as pleasant as the blessed manna that rained from Heaven among the Israelites."

When the Israelites were wandering in the desert, they ate manna, aka bread from Heaven.

Exodus 16:15 states, "*And when the children of Israel saw it, they said one to another, It is Manna, for they wist not what it was. And Moses said unto them, This is the bread which the Lord hath given you to eat*" (1599 Geneva Bible).

Leir added, "It has recalled my spirits home again and made me as fresh as I was before. But how shall we thank them for their kindness?"

"Truly, I don't know how we can sufficiently thank them," Perillus said, "but the best way that I can think of is this: I'll offer them my jacket in requital, for we have nothing else to spare."

"No, don't, Perillus, for they shall have mine," Leir said.

"Pardon me, my lord, but I swear they shall have mine," Perillus said.

He offered the disguised Cordella and the others his jacket, but they would not take it.

"Ah, who would think such kindness should remain among such foreign and unacquainted men," Leir said, "and that such hate should harbor in the breast of those who have reason to be best?"

"Ah, good old father, tell me your grief," the disguised Cordella said. "I'll sorrow with you if not add relief."

"Ah, good young daughter, I may call you so," Leir said, "for you are like a daughter whom I had."

"Don't you have her still?" the disguised Cordella asked. "Is she dead?"

"No, God forbid, but all of my claim to call her my daughter is gone because I acted too much unnatural and not like a father," Leir said. "So I have lost the title of a father and may instead be called a stranger to her."

"Your title of a father is good still," the disguised Cordella said, "for it is always known that a man may do as he wishes with his own. But have you then only one daughter in all?"

"I have more daughters by two than I wish I had," Leir said.

"Oh, don't say that, but instead see the result in the end," the disguised Cordella said. "They who are bad may have the grace to mend. But how have they offended you so much?"

"If from the first I should relate the cause, it would make a heart made of hard adamant weep," Leir said, "and you, poor soul, kind-hearted as you are, weep already before I begin."

"For God's love tell it," the disguised Cordella said, "and when you have finished, I'll tell you the reason why I weep so soon."

"Then know this first," Leir said. "I am a Briton born, and I had three daughters by one loving wife, and although it is I their father saying it, of beauty they were well endowed, especially the youngest of the three, for her perfections hardly matched could be.

"On these daughters I doted with a jealous love and thought to test who of them loved me best by asking them who would do most for me.

"The first and second flattered me with words and vowed that they loved me better than their lives.

"The youngest said she loved me as a child might do. Her answer I esteemed most vile and immediately, in an outrageous mood, I turned her from me to go and either sink or swim, and all I had, even to the very clothes, I gave in dowry to the other two daughters, and she — the youngest daughter — who best deserved the greatest share, I gave nothing but disgrace and worries, aka cares.

"Now mark the sequel: When I had done thus, I sojourned in my eldest daughter's house where, for a time, I was treated well and lived in a way that was suitable for my position. But every day her kindness grew cold, which I with patience put up with well enough, and pretended not to see the things I saw. But at last she grew so far incensed with moody fury and with causeless hate that, in most vile and contumelious terms, she bade me to go packing and harbor somewhere else.

"Then was I obliged for refuge to journey to my second oldest daughter for relief. She gave me pleasing and most courteous words, but in her actions showed herself to be as harsh and cruel as never any daughter did before. She asked me to go early in a morning out to a thicket two miles from the court, saying that there she would come and talk with me. But there she had set a shaggy-haired murdering wretch to massacre my honest friend and me.

"So then judge for yourself, although my tale is brief, whether man ever had greater cause for grief."

"Never was like impiety done since the creation of the world was begun," the King of Gallia said.

"And now I am constrained to seek relief from my youngest daughter to whom I have been so unkind," Leir said, "whose censure, if it awards me death, I must confess she pays me but what is my due.

"But if she will show me a loving daughter's part, it comes from God and her, not from my merit and desert."

"No doubt she will treat you well," the disguised Cordella said. "I dare be sworn she will."

"How can you know that, since you don't know who she is?" Leir asked.

"I myself have a father a great way from here," the disguised Cordella said, "who treated me as badly as ever you did her, yet if I once might see his reverend old age, I'd creep along to meet him on my knee."

"Oh, no men's children are unkind but mine," Leir said.

"Don't condemn all because of others' crimes," the disguised Cordella said. "But look, dear father, look, behold and see, it is your loving daughter who is speaking to you."

She removed part of her disguise and knelt.

"Oh, stand up!" Leir said. "It is my part to kneel and ask forgiveness for my former faults."

Leir knelt.

"Oh, if you wish I should enjoy my breath, dear father rise, or else I receive my death," Cordella said.

Leir rose and said, "Then I will rise, to satisfy your mind, but then kneel again, until my pardon is granted."

Leir knelt.

"I pardon you," Cordella said. "The word is not fitting for me to say, but I say it in order to ease your knee. You gave me life; you were the reason that I am what I am, who otherwise would have never been."

"But you gave life to me and to my friend," Leir replied, "whose days had otherwise had an untimely end."

"You brought me up when I was but young," Cordella said, "and much unable to help myself."

"I cast you forth when you were but young and much unable to help yourself," Leir said.

"God, world, and nature say I am doing you wrong," Cordella said, "I who can endure to see you kneel so long."

"Let me break off this loving controversy," the King of Gallia said, "which makes my very soul rejoice to see. Good father-in-law, rise. She is your loving daughter."

Leir rose.

The King of Gallia continued, "She honors you with the same respectful reverence that she would if you were the monarch of the world."

Cordella knelt and said, "But I will never rise from off my knee, until I have your blessing and your pardon for all my faults I have committed in any way from the first moment of my birth to this present day."

"May the blessing that the God of Abraham gave to the tribe of Judah alight on you," Leir said, "and multiply your days, so that you may see your children's children prosper after you."

That blessing can be found in Genesis 12:2-3 (1599 Geneva Bible):

2 And I will make of thee a great nation, and will bless thee, and make thy name great, and thou shalt be a blessing.

3 I will also bless them that bless thee, and curse them that curse thee, and in thee shall all families of the earth be blessed.

Leir continued, "Your faults, which are just none that I know of, may God pardon on high, and I forgive below."

Cordella rose and said, "Now is my heart at peace. It leaps within my breast for joy of this good chance meeting. And now, dear father, welcome to our court, and you are welcome, kind Perillus, you model of virtue and true honesty."

"Oh, Perillus has been the kindest friend to me that a man ever had in adversity," Leir said.

"My tongue fails to say what my heart does think," Perillus said. "I am so overcome with exceeding joy."

"All of you have spoken," the King of Gallia said, "so now let me speak my mind, and in few words much matter here conclude."

He knelt and said, "If ever my heart harbors any joy or if true happiness reposes within my breast before I have rooted out this viperous sect and repossessed my father-in-law of his crown, let me be counted for the most perjured man who has ever spoken a word since the world began."

The King of Gallia rose.

Mumford said, "Let me pray, too, although I am a man who has never prayed before."

He knelt and prayed, "If ever I regret and return to the British earth, as, before much longer, I presume I shall, and return from thence without my wench, let me be gelded for my recompense."

"Gelded" means "castrated."

Mumford rose.

The King of Gallia said, "Come, let's go to arms to redress this wrong. Until I am there in England with an army, I think the time seems long."

— 5.5 —

— Scene 25 —

Alone, Ragan talked to herself:

"I feel a hell of conscience in my breast, tormenting me with horror for my crime, and it makes me feel an agony of fear, out of fear the world should find my dealing out.

"I have never set eye upon the peasant slave whom I appointed for the crime since. Oh, if I could get to him to make him sure — to kill him and make sure that he tells no one what I ordered him to do — my fear would cease, and I would rest secure.

90

"But if the old men — Leir and Perillus — with some persuasive words have saved their lives and convinced him to relent and not kill them, then the old men have fled to the court of France, and like a trumpet are revealing my shame.

"A shame on these white-livered, cowardly slaves, say I, who so soon are overcome with fair words. Oh, God, if I had been but made a man, or if my strength were equal with my will! These foolish men are nothing but pure pity, and they melt like butter melts in the sun. Why should they have pre-eminence over us women, since we are creatures of braver resolve?

"I swear, I am quite out of charity with all the heartless men in Christendom. A pox upon them when they are afraid to give a stab or slit a paltry windpipe, which are such easy actions to do.

"Well, if I had thought the slave would treat me like this, I myself would have been the executioner. That is now impossible, and if my intended deed is known, I'll make as good shift as I can to save myself.

"He who complains at me however this matter stands, it would be best for him to keep himself away from my hands."

— 5.6 —

— Scene 26 —

Military drums and trumpets sounded among the Gallian army, which was at a port in Gallia. The King of Gallia, Leir, and Mumford talked together.

The King of Gallia said, "Thus have we brought our army to the sea where our ships are ready to receive us. The wind stands fair, and we in four hours' sailing may easily arrive on the British shore, where, unexpected, we may surprise them and gain a glorious victory with ease.

"Therefore, my loving countrymen, resolve, since truth and justice fight on our sides, that we shall march and conquer where we go.

"I myself will be as far forward in the battle as the soldiers in the first line, and I will march step by step with the hardiest fellow, and the meanest soldier in our camp shall not be in danger, but I'll second him — I will support and reinforce him."

Using the royal plural, he then said to Mumford, "To you, my lord, we give the whole command of all the army, second only to ourself. I have no doubt that you will fight with your usual valor in this needful case, encouraging the rest to do the like by your proven lofty courage."

"My liege," Mumford said, "it isn't necessary to spur a willing horse that's apt enough to run himself to death, for here I swear by that sweet Saint Denis' bright eyes that are the stars that guide me to good fortune, either to see my old lord Leir crowned anew, or in his cause to bid the world adieu."

"Thanks, good Lord Mumford," Leir said. "Your fighting is caused more by your good will than by any merit or desert in me."

Mumford said to the soldiers, "And now to you, my worthy countrymen, you valiant race of Genovestan Gauls from Orleans, surnamed Redshanks for your chivalry, because you fight up to the shanks in red blood, show yourselves now to be true Gauls indeed, and be so bitter to your enemies that they may say you are as bitter as gall.

"Gall them, brave shooters, with your artillery. Gall them, brave halberds, with your sharp-pointed bills, aka spear-heads, each in their pointed and appointed place. Gall them, and Gaul them.

"Not one, but all, fight for the credit of yourselves and Gaul."

The King of Gallia said, "What more persuasion is needed by those who rather wish to deal blows than to hear of blows? Let's go onboard our ships. And if God permits, in four hours' sail I hope we shall be there."

"And in five hours more," Mumford said, "I have no doubt but we shall bring our wished-for desires about."

— 5.7 —

— Scene 27 —

An English Captain of the watch and two English watchmen talked together. The Captain was giving the two watchmen their orders: They were to stay in the watchtower and light a beacon — a fire — if they saw the enemy approaching. Lighting a beacon was called firing a beacon.

"My honest friends," the English Captain said, "it is your turn tonight to watch in this place, near about the beacon, and vigilantly watch in case any fleet of ships comes here. If you see the enemies' ships, your duty is to fire the beacon immediately and wake up the people in the town."

The first watchman said, "Yes, yes, yes, fear nothing. We know our responsibility, I warrant."

The English Captain exited.

The first watchman said to the second watchman, "I have been a watchman about this beacon these past thirty years, and yet I have never seen any trouble but have always stood watch as quietly as might be."

"Indeed, neighbor," the second watchman said, "if you'll follow my vice and advice, instead of watching at the beacon, we'll go to Goodman Jennings' inn and watch a pot of ale and a rasher of bacon. And if we do not drink ourselves drunk, then so, I warrant, the beacon will see us when we come out again."

"Yes," the first watchman said, "but what if somebody excuse us to the Captain?"

He had made a malapropism: "excuse" instead of "accuse."

"That doesn't matter," the second watchman said. "I'll prove by good reason that we watch the beacon, ass for example —"

"I hope you aren't calling me 'ass' on purpose, neighbor," the first watchman said.

"No, no," the second watchman said, "but for example, let's say that here stands the pot of ale — that's the beacon."

"Yes, yes, it is a very good beacon," the first watchman said.

"Well, let's say that here stands your nose — that's the fire," the second watchman said.

"Indeed, I must confess that my nose is somewhat red," the first watchman said.

"Let's say that I see come marching in a dish, half a score pieces of salt bacon," the second watchman said.

A score is twenty, so half a score is ten.

"I understand your meaning," the first watchman said. "That's as much to say half a score ships sailing on the salty sea."

"True," the second watchman said. "You understand me correctly. Immediately, like a faithful watchman, I fire the beacon and call up the town."

"Yes," the first watchman said,. "In other words, you set your nose to the pot, and drink up the drink."

"You are in the right," the second watchman said. "Come, let's go fire the beacon."

— 5.8 —

— Scene 28 —

The Gallian soldiers were marching to a muffled drum as the King of Gallia spoke to Mumford and the soldiers.

"Now our banners march on the British earth, and we are approaching close to the town. Then look about you, valiant countrymen, and we shall finish this exploit with ease. The inhabitants of this suspicious place are dead asleep, like men who are sure that they are safe.

"Here shall we skirmish only with naked men — half-dressed because they were not expecting a battle — who won't know what our coming portends until they feel our meaning on their skins.

"Therefore, attack! God and our right for us! Right is on our side."

— 5.9 —

— Scene 29 —

The town was surprised — attacked with warning —because the two watchmen had neglected their duty and had gotten drunk. Now, military trumpets sounded, and half-dressed English soldiers and half-dressed English women were running around.

Two English Captains, carrying swords but not wearing their usual jackets, met.

The first Captain, who was the one who had given the two watchmen their orders, said, "Where are these villains who were supposed to watch and fire the beacon, if the need arose, but who have through neglect of their duty allowed us to be surprised because they never gave notice of the approaching enemy soldiers to the town? We are betrayed and quite devoid of hope by any means to fortify ourselves."

"It is ten to one that the peasants are drunk and asleep," the second Captain said, "and so they neglect their responsibility."

"May a whirlwind carry them quickly to a whirlpool," the first Captain said, "so that there the slaves may drink their bellies full."

"This is what happens when the beacon is so near the ale house," the second Captain said.

The two watchmen arrived; they were drunk, and each was carrying a tankard of ale.

"Damn you, villains!" the first Captain said. "Where are you running now?"

"To fire the town and call up the beacon," the first watchman said.

He was so drunk that he had gotten his words mixed up: He had said that he was going to set fire to the town and wake up the beacon.

"No, no, sir," the second watchman said. "We are going to fire the beacon."

He drank.

"What, with a pot of ale, you drunken rogues?" the second Captain said.

"You'll fire the beacon after the town has been lost!" the first Captain said. "I'll teach you how to tend to your office better."

He drew his sword to stab the second watchman.

Mumford arrived on the scene, and the two English Captains ran away.

"Yield, yield, yield!" Mumford cried, knocking down the two watchmen's tankards of ale.

"Reel?" the first watchman said. "No, we do not reel. You may lack a pot of ale before you die."

"But in the meantime, I answer that you lack none," Mumford said, seeing that they were drunk. He added sarcastically, "Well, there's no dealing with you. You are 'well-built' and 'well-weaponed' men. I wish that there were no 'worse' than you in the town."

He exited.

"He speaks like an honest man," the second watchman said. "My anger has passed already. Come, neighbor, let's go."

"No," the first watchman said. "First, let's see if we can stand."

They exited. Almost immediately, Mumford chased some half-naked English soldiers across the place where the two watchmen had been.

— 5.10 —

— Scene 30 —

The King of Gallia, Leir, Mumford, Cordella, Perillus, and some Gallian soldiers stood together. Also present were the Chief of the town, bound, and an English nobleman.

"Fear not, my friends," the King of Gallia said, "you shall receive no hurt if you'll recognize and serve your lawful king and entirely revoke your fealty from the King of Cambria, and from the aspiring King of Cornwall, too, whose wives have practiced treason against their father's life.

"We come seeking justice for your wronged, rightful king, and we intend no harm at all to you, as long as you submit to your lawful king."

"Kind countrymen," Leir said, "it grieves me that by necessity I am constrained to use extreme measures to regain my crown."

"Long have you here been looked for, my good lord, and wished for by a general consent of your subjects," the English nobleman said. "And if we had known that your highness had arrived, we would not have made any resistance to your grace."

According to the English nobleman, he and others had fought because they did not know that France was invading England on behalf of Leir.

The English nobleman continued, "And now, my gracious lord, you need not doubt that all the country will yield immediately. Your country, since your absence, has been greatly taxed in order to maintain the over-swelling pride of Gonorill and Ragan and their husbands, all of whom required many expensive goods.

"We'll immediately send word of your arrival to all our friends. When they have notice, they will come quickly to swear their loyalty to you."

"Thanks, loving subjects," Leir said, "and thanks, worthy son-in-law. Thanks, my kind daughter. Thanks to you, Mumford, my lord, who willingly risked half your blood to do me so much good without my deserving it."

"Oh, don't say that!" Mumford said. "I have been much beholden to your grace. I must confess that I have been in some skirmishes, but I was never in the like to this, for where I was accustomed to meet with armed men, I was just now encountered by naked women."

The town had been surprised, and its men and women had been only half dressed.

Leir and the forces on his side had taken the English town, but the armies of the King of Cambria and the King of Cornwall were coming, and quickly a major battle would be fought.

"We who are feeble and lack the use of weapons will pray to God to shield you from all harms," Cordella said.

"While all your hands engage in ceaseless toil," Leir said, "our hearts shall pray that the foes may suffer defeat."

"While you fight for us," Perillus said, "We'll fast and pray that victory may pursue what is just and right."

"I think your words make my muscles grow bigger, my friends, and your words add fresh vigor to my willing limbs," the King of Gallia said.

Military drums sounded.

"But listen," the King of Gallia added. "I hear the enemy drums approach. God and our right, Saint Denis, and Saint George!"

Saint Denis is the patron saint of France, and Saint George is the patron saint of England.

The King of Cornwall, the King of Cambria, Gonorill, Ragan, and some of their soldiers arrived.

"Presumptuous King of the Gauls, how dare you presume to step on our British shore?" the King of Cornwall said. "And, more than that, to take our towns by force, and draw our subjects' hearts from their true king? Be sure that you will buy it at as dear a price as ever you bought presumption in your lives."

"Over-daring Cornwall, know that we came here to get right and just revenge for the wronged King of England, whose daughters there, fell vipers as they are, have sought to murder and deprive him of life," the King of Gallia said. "But God protected him from all their spite, and we have come here in the justice of his right."

"Neither he nor you has any interest here except what you win and purchase with the sword," the King of Cambria said. "We will thrust your slanders to our noble virtuous queens down your throat in the battle unless, out of fear of our revenging hands, you flee to the sea, knowing that you are not safe on our lands."

"Welshman," Mumford said, "before night I'll so viciously attack you like a ferret attacks a rat for those words that you shall have no mind to boast as well for the next year."

"Those who say that we sought our father's death lie," Gonorill said.

"That charge was entirely made up in order to provide an excuse — one with the appearance of justice — for you to invade England,"

Ragan said. "I think that an old man who is getting ready to die should be ashamed to declare publicly so foul a lie."

"For shame, shameless sister, so devoid of grace, that you call our father 'liar' to his face," Cordella said.

Gonorill replied, "Shut up, you Puritan, you dissembling hypocrite, who are so 'good' that you will prove to be completely evil! Soon, when I have you in my fingers, I'll make you wish yourself in Purgatory."

"Be quiet, you monster, shame to your sex," Perillus said. "You fiend in the likeness of a human creature!"

"I have never heard a fouler-spoken man," Ragan said.

"Damn you, viper, scum, filthy parricide," Leir said. "You are more odious to my sight than is a toad."

He showed her a letter — the letter authorizing his murder — and then he asked her, "Do you know this letter?"

She grabbed the letter and tore it up, saying, "Do you think to outface me with your paltry letter? Using the pretext of a forged letter, you have come to drive my husband from his rightful place as ruler."

"Has anyone ever heard impiety as bad as this?" Leir asked.

Perillus said to Ragan, "You owe us more patience than this because we have shown you patience. We were more patient when we waited for you within the thicket two long hours and more."

"What hours?" Ragan said. "What thicket?"

Perillus replied, "The thicket where you sent your servant with your letter, sealed with your hand, ordering him to send us both to Heaven, where, I think, you never mean to come."

"Alas, you are grown a child again because of your old age, or else your senses dote for lack of sleep," Ragan said.

"Indeed, you made us rise early, you know," Perillus said, "yet you tried to take care that we should sleep where you bade us wait for you, but you wanted us to never wake up anymore until the latter day — the Day of Judgment."

"Peace, peace, old fellow," Gonorill said. "You are sleepy still."

"Indeed," Mumford said to Perillus, "even if you argue with them until tomorrow, you will get no other answer at their hands. It is a pity that two such good faces should have so little grace between them. Well, let us see if the husbands can do as much with their hands as they — the wives — do with their tongues."

"Yes, with their swords they'll make your tongues unsay what they have said, or else they'll cut them out," the King of Cambria said.

"Let's go to it, gallants," the King of Gallia said. "Let's go to battle. Let's not stand around brawling like this."

Everyone exited to arrange the armies for battle.

— 5.11 —

— Scene 31 —

In the battle, Mumford chased after the King of Cambria, who fled from him.

On the battlefield, the King of Cornwall said, "The day is lost. Our 'friends' all revolt against us and join against us with our enemies. There is no means of safety except by flight, and therefore I'll flee to Cornwall with my queen."

He exited.

The King of Cambria entered the scene and said, "I think there is a devil in their camp who has been haunting me today. He has so tired me that in a manner I can fight no more."

Mumford arrived on the scene.

Seeing him, the King of Cambria said, "By God's wounds, here he comes; I'll take me to my horse."

He ran away.

Mumford chased him, but the King of Cambria succeeded in outrunning him and reaching his horse.

Mumford said, "Farewell, Welshman. I give you what is your due: You have a light and nimble pair of legs. You are more in debt to them than you are to your hands, but if I meet you once again today, I'll cut them off and graft them on to someone with a better heart."

100

The military trumpets announced victory for Leir and the King of Gallia. Leir, Perillus, the King of Gallia, Cordella, and Mumford talked together.

The King of Gallia said to Leir, "Thanks be to God, your foes are overcome, and you are again possessed of your right."

"I give thanks first to the Heavens," Leir said, "and next, I give thanks to you, my son-in-law, by whose good means I repossess my right, which if it please you to accept it for yourself, with all my heart I will resign it to you, for it is yours by right, and none of mine.

"First, you have raised, at your own charge, an army of valiant soldiers — this comes all from you.

"Next you have ventured and risked your own body in battle.

"And lastly, worthy, morally unblemished King of Gallia, I have regained my kingly title because of you."

"Thank the Heavens, not me," the King of Gallia replied. "My zeal to you is such that you can command all I have, and I will never complain."

"He who with all kind love treats his queen will not be seen to be to her father unkind," Cordella said.

"Ah, my Cordella, now I remember your modest answer that I took to be unkind," Leir said, "but now that I can see clearly, I am not even a little deceived. I know that you loved and love me dearly, and as ought a child.

"And you, Perillus, once my partner in woe, you to requite, the best I can, I'll do. Yet all that I can do to requite you — no matter how much it is — would not be sufficient because your love for me is so true."

"Thanks, worthy Mumford, to you last of all. You are not greeted last because your desert was small — your merit is great. You have like a lion laid blows on the enemy today, chasing the King of Cornwall and the King of Cambria, who with my daughters — 'daughters,' did I say? — to save their lives, ran away like fugitives.

"Come, son-in-law and daughter, who did advance me to my kingship again, stay with me awhile, and then leave for France."

APPENDIX A: BIBLIOGRAPHY

The History of King Leir **(Modern Language)**

Author: Anonymous

Editor: Andrew Griffin

This version has notes (each Chapter is on a different screen):

http://internetshakespeare.uvic.ca/doc/Leir _M/scene/1/

This version is without notes:

http://internetshakespeare.uvic.ca/doc/Leir _M/complete/

The History of King Leir **(Table of Contents, and Links to Various Sections)**

http://qme.internetshakespeare.uvic.ca//Library/Texts/Leir /

The History of King Leir **(Quarto)**

Author: Anonymous

Editors: Andrew Griffin

http://internetshakespeare.uvic.ca/doc/Leir _Q1/complete/

NOTE: The above links are for the Queen's Men Editions.

Published by the Internet Shakespeare Editions. This site is supported by the University of Victoria and the Social Sciences and Humanities Research Council of Canada.

OTHER WORKS

Everitt, E.B. and R.L. Armstrong (for *Edward III*). *Six Early Plays Related to the Shakespeare Canon*. Copenhagen, Rosenkilde and Bagger, 1965.

Michie, Donald M. *A Critical Edition of* The true chronicle history of King Leir and his three daughters, Gonorill, Ragan and Cordella. New York: Garland Publishing, Inc., 1991.

Stern, Tiffany, editor. *King Leir.* New York: Routledge, 2003, c2002.

APPENDIX B: ABOUT THE AUTHOR

It was a dark and stormy night. Suddenly a cry rang out, and on a hot summer night in 1954, Josephine, wife of Carl Bruce, gave birth to a boy — me. Unfortunately, this young married couple allowed Reuben Saturday, Josephine's brother, to name their first-born. Reuben, aka "The Joker," decided that Bruce was a nice name, so he decided to name me Bruce Bruce. I have gone by my middle name — David — ever since.

Being named Bruce David Bruce hasn't been all bad. Bank tellers remember me very quickly, so I don't often have to show an ID. It can be fun in charades, also. When I was a counselor as a teenager at Camp Echoing Hills in Warsaw, Ohio, a fellow counselor gave the signs for "sounds like" and "two words," then she pointed to a bruise on her leg twice. Bruise Bruise? Oh yeah, Bruce Bruce is the answer!

Uncle Reuben, by the way, gave me a haircut when I was in kindergarten. He cut my hair short and shaved a small bald spot on the back of my head. My mother wouldn't let me go to school until the bald spot grew out again.

Of all my brothers and sisters (six in all), I am the only transplant to Athens, Ohio. I was born in Newark, Ohio, and have lived all around Southeastern Ohio. However, I moved to Athens to go to Ohio University and have never left.

At Ohio U, I never could make up my mind whether to major in English or Philosophy, so I got a bachelor's degree with a double major in both areas, then I added a master's degree in English and a master's degree in Philosophy.

Currently, and for a long time to come (I eat fruits and vegetables), I am spending my retirement writing books such as *Nadia Comaneci: Perfect 10*, *The Funniest People in Dance*, *Homer's* Iliad: *A Retelling in Prose*, and *William Shakespeare's* Othello: *A Retelling in Prose*.

By the way, my sister Brenda Kennedy writes romances such as *A New Beginning* and *Shattered Dreams*.

APPENDIX C: SOME BOOKS BY DAVID BRUCE

Retellings of a Classic Work of Literature

Arden of Faversham: *A Retelling*

Ben Jonson's The Alchemist: *A Retelling*

Ben Jonson's The Arraignment, or Poetaster: *A Retelling*

Ben Jonson's Bartholomew Fair: *A Retelling*

Ben Jonson's The Case is Altered: *A Retelling*

Ben Jonson's Catiline's Conspiracy: *A Retelling*

Ben Jonson's The Devil is an Ass: *A Retelling*

Ben Jonson's Epicene: *A Retelling*

Ben Jonson's Every Man in His Humor: *A Retelling*

Ben Jonson's Every Man Out of His Humor: *A Retelling*

Ben Jonson's The Fountain of Self-Love, or Cynthia's Revels: *A Retelling*

Ben Jonson's The Magnetic Lady, or Humors Reconciled: *A Retelling*

Ben Jonson's The New Inn, or The Light Heart: *A Retelling*

Ben Jonson's Sejanus' Fall: *A Retelling*

Ben Jonson's The Staple of News: *A Retelling*

Ben Jonson's A Tale of a Tub: *A Retelling*

Ben Jonson's Volpone, or the Fox: *A Retelling*

Christopher Marlowe's Complete Plays: Retellings

Christopher Marlowe's Dido, Queen of Carthage: *A Retelling*

Christopher Marlowe's Doctor Faustus: *Retellings of the 1604 A-Text and of the 1616 B-Text*

Christopher Marlowe's Edward II: *A Retelling*

Christopher Marlowe's The Massacre at Paris: *A Retelling*

Christopher Marlowe's The Rich Jew of Malta: *A Retelling*

Christopher Marlowe's Tamburlaine, Parts 1 and 2: *Retellings*

Dante's Divine Comedy: *A Retelling in Prose*

Dante's Inferno: *A Retelling in Prose*

Dante's Purgatory: *A Retelling in Prose*

Dante's Paradise: *A Retelling in Prose*

The Famous Victories of Henry V: *A Retelling*

From the Iliad *to the* Odyssey: *A Retelling in Prose of Quintus of Smyrna's* Posthomerica

George Chapman, Ben Jonson, and John Marston's Eastward Ho! *A Retelling*

William Shakespeare's The Tempest: *A Retelling in Prose*
William Shakespeare's Timon of Athens: *A Retelling in Prose*
William Shakespeare's Titus Andronicus: *A Retelling in Prose*
William Shakespeare's Troilus and Cressida: *A Retelling in Prose*
William Shakespeare's Twelfth Night: *A Retelling in Prose*
William Shakespeare's The Two Gentlemen of Verona: *A Retelling in Prose*
William Shakespeare's The Two Noble Kinsmen: *A Retelling in Prose*
William Shakespeare's The Winter's Tale: *A Retelling in Prose*